When Emily Sinclair discovers that deckchair attendant James Bradshaw is two-timing her with Madame Zora, she sprays the details in brilliant pink paint outside the fortune-teller's caravan. It's six years before Emily sees James again and she realises that she still loves him. The only trouble is, James has purchased the Victorian playhouse theatre she manages and, unless she can turn its fortune around, he is threatening to close it down.

MS

MARGARET MOUNSDON

MEMORIES OF LOVE

Complete and Unabridged

LINFORD
Leicester

First published in Great Britain in 2010

First Linford Edition
published 2011

British Library CIP Data

Mounsdon, Margaret.
  Memories of love. - -
  (Linford romance library)
  1. Love stories.
  2. Large type books.
  I. Title II. Series
  823.9′2–dc22

  ISBN 978–1–4448–0849–0

Published by
F. A. Thorpe (Publishing)
Anstey, Leicestershire

Set by Words & Graphics Ltd.
Anstey, Leicestershire
Printed and bound in Great Britain by
T. J. International Ltd., Padstow, Cornwall

This book is printed on acid-free paper

'The Little Alhambra Is Your Life'

'So there you have it.' Joe Sykes cleared his throat. When Emily made no response, he continued, 'I leave at the end of the month and the new man will take over on the first.'

He leaned back in his chair a look of apprehension on his face.

'You've sold The Little Alhambra?' Emily repeated in amazement. Joe's announcement hadn't exactly come as a bombshell, but it had taken her breath away.

There had been rumours buzzing around backstage for some time now. Although Emily did not generally join in Green Room gossip she suspected the latest stories did hold a grain of truth. What she had not suspected was that negotiations were so far advanced.

'I know it will come as something of a shock, Emily, and I wanted to let you know before now, but I had no choice. I was legally sworn to secrecy until the contracts were signed.'

'But why?' Emily knew the answer to her question but her head wouldn't accept it. 'We've had our ups and downs before but we've always pulled through.'

Joe's outdoor complexion, ruddy from years of sailing, deepened in colour. From the expression on his face Emily could tell he wasn't enjoying this interview any more than she was. He was a man who hated confrontation of any sort, a man who would rather walk barefoot over cut glass than have an argument.

'We are losing money hand over fist. You know that, Emily. Things could not continue as they were. If I hadn't found a suitable buyer for the old place then the only other option would have been total closure.'

It was hot in the tiny back room,

rather grandly referred to as the office. On stifling days like today it resembled more of an overheated broom cupboard than the nerve centre of a busy theatre. Through the open window Emily could hear the seagulls keening overhead hoping to swoop on the day's catch as it was landed on the quay.

Early afternoon was one of the busiest times of the day on the seafront at West Hampton, especially at the beginning of the summer season, when all the chefs, anxious to provide the freshest seafood for their evening menus, vied with each other for the best deals on that day's catch.

The slightly faded seaside resort of West Hampton was fast becoming popular with the fashionable set. Some of the older properties a few miles inland had been snapped up by minor celebrities and several new gourmet eateries had opened on the esplanade jostling for space alongside the older more established, traditional hotels.

'The Little Alhambra is your life,

Joe,' Emily said.

'And yours,' Joe added quietly. 'You hardly ever take a day off.'

Emily loved what she did and on Mondays, when the theatre was dark, she liked to catch up with the mountain of paperwork that never seemed to diminish. It was easier to try to attack it, without the constant interruptions that were part of her job as manager.

She had been surprised to find Joe Sykes seated at his desk. His wife, Maisie, encouraged him to have at least one clear day off a week besides Sunday and she did not like having her plans disrupted by theatre work.

'Last winter wasn't easy, what with the leaky roof and the Health and Safety people on my back. The refurbishment costs were a killer. I'm still not happy about the plumbing. Some of the pipes are original and I don't know how much longer they'll last out,' Joe began to explain. 'I'm not getting any younger, Emily, and Maisie has a fancy to spend more time with the grandchildren. She's been such a support over the years, I feel I owe it to her to retire now while I still have my health.'

'I understand that, Joe,' Emily nodded, her sympathies with Maisie, 'but there's always been a theatre here since as long as anyone can remember.'

'And there still will be. By signing that contract I've granted the old place a reprieve.'

Emily wasn't so sure. Developers had been after the land for years and Joe had provided them with the opportunity they were looking for.

'What about the rest of the team?' Emily was thinking of the other two full-time members of staff. Ivy who ran the tearoom and bar, and her husband, Ted, the odd job man. They had been here for years and Emily didn't dare think how the change would affect their lives, or those of the numerous part-time workers who ensured the smooth running of every production. 'Have you told them?'

'Not yet, I wanted you to be the first to know.'

'I see.'

Emily looked out of the window again to where an aircraft scarred the brilliant sky with a white vapour trail. She knew she was the luckiest person in the world to be doing a job she absolutely adored. Would she too have to move to one of the big towns and work in a noisy open plan office? The prospect filled her with dread.

She could not imagine ever leaving her cramped fisherman's cottage down by the harbour. Every morning she awoke to the sound of the waves lapping the seashore and the smell of salt air flapping the curtains through her open window. She loved the walk up the hill to the quaint theatre perched on the hilltop at the top of the town. It was a local landmark and if it closed it would be a vicious blow to the local community.

'I'm sure everyone's job will be safe,' Joe said, doing his best to reassure her.

'Only if the new owner keeps the theatre on as a going concern.'

'I've no reason to believe he won't and I've given you all glowing references.'

'Do you think he will, keep the theatre going I mean?' Emily asked, still feeling sick in the pit of her stomach.

She had worked at the theatre for three years now, first of all as a temporary programme seller when she could get no other job. Her duties entailed doing the running around for everyone and then when one of the box office agents retired, she moved up to front of house.

Then after a bad bout of flu and at Maisie's insistence, Joe had relinquished more of his responsibilities and promoted Emily to manager. Eventually he had handed over total responsibility of the day-to-day running of the theatre to her and once he had ascertained Emily's suitability for the position, he more or less left her to get on with it.

It was a dream job. No two days were

the same and Emily loved the challenge of making things happen. There was no greater thrill than watching chaos turn to order as a new production came to life.

So what if they weren't making a healthy profit? It was the lifeblood of the community, a focal point. At some time in their lives everyone in West Hampton had visited The Little Alhambra.

The senior bus would roll onto the forecourt regular as clockwork for the Wednesday matinee. Even though the patrons had enjoyed a substantial fish and chip lunch on the pier, Emily always made sure there was a plentiful supply of sweet tea and biscuits for them. For some it was their only outing of the week and she knew how much everyone cherished their visits.

Children loved the Saturday morning specials when all sorts of interactive entertainment was offered from spaceships to singalongs. Parents valued the chance to get their offspring away from computer games and were totally supportive of every new venture.

Then there were the plays themselves. The Little Alhambra put on everything from thrillers to musicals, farces, the classics, a pantomime and contemporary modern plays. Emily always made sure the programme was varied enough to appeal to everyone's tastes.

'I had to deal with Mr Bradshaw's agent as he's out of the country at the moment, but he has assured me Mr Bradshaw wants things to continue normally for the time being,' Joe replied to her question.

Emily blinked hard and tried not to sway, but nothing eased the buzzing in her ears. She knew Joe would not have taken this action unless it had been forced on him and in his position she had to admit she might have made the same decision, but this latest realisation that she might be in deep trouble did not make the blow any easier to bear.

'Thanks to your excellent organisational skills we have a good provisional programme scheduled for the summer season and the forward bookings are showing promise. I'm sure they'll pick up once the holiday makers start arriving.'

'Did you say the new owner was called Mr Bradshaw?' Emily asked carefully.

'Yes.'

'Would that be James Bradshaw?' The question stuck in Emily's throat and it was only with the greatest of difficulty that she managed to speak his name.

'Yes.' Joe smiled for the first time since he had called her into the office. 'You know him, don't you?'

'Yes. I knew him.' Emily did her best to keep her voice normal.

'His agent tells me he spent a summer down here a few years ago, I can't remember exactly how many.'

'It was six years ago,' Emily said, her voice now little more than a whisper.

'That when you bumped into him,

was it?' Joe's hearing wasn't all it should be and he didn't appear to have caught Emily's interruption. 'He had a holiday job, something on the seafront I believe.'

'He rented out the deckchairs.'

'You'll be able to catch up on old times then, won't you?' Joe was now looking a lot happier. 'I believe he's done rather well for himself after he got his business degree. He owns several similar properties to ours, all along the south coast. Admittedly some have been converted to cinemas, but I don't think that's what he has in mind for The Little Alhambra.' Joe ground to a halt aware that Emily's attention had wandered.

'Emily, is something wrong?' he asked.

'Nothing at all,' Emily replied, doing her best to smile. 'It's been a bit of a shock, that's all. I'm sure you've made the right decision, Joe.'

'I wanted to tell you what was going on when I first started negotiations, but that wasn't possible, then with the time difference between here and America, the deal wasn't finalised until midday today our time and there was a clause in the contract forbidding me to reveal any of the details beforehand.'

'I understand, Joe. I'm sure you've done the right thing. Do you mind if I go outside for a breath of fresh air?' Emily asked.

'Of course not. Take the rest of the day off. The paperwork can wait,' Joe insisted. 'We're dark tonight so I'll lock up on my way out if you like.'

The main doors were open and the warm April breeze wafting through them cleared Emily's head as she walked across the creaky floored foyer, past the retro style booking office and the posters advertising the new play, a contemporary drama, due to start later in the week.

There had always been a theatre in Alhambra Place for as long as anyone could remember and if Emily had anything to do with it, The Little

Alhambra was not going down without a fight.

She paused on the outside steps and took a deep breath of bracing sea air.

It was a tradition that Mondays were always The Little Alhambra's dark night. It gave Ted and Ivy a day off and if a new production was scheduled, the cast had time to get down to West Hampton, settle in to their lodgings, rehearse and attend to the other numerous details that needed to be seen to at the beginning of every run.

But today Emily didn't want to think about any of that. Even if she didn't want to, she had to think about James Bradshaw.

Would he remember her? It had been six years since she had last seen him. Emily began to walk down the cobble-stoned hill that led towards the seafront. She certainly remembered him.

James Bradshaw had been a deck-chair attendant. He had worked for Benito's Entertainments. Benito ran the seafront fun fair and every Sunday afternoon he also arranged a brass band concert in the bandstand. They were extremely popular and there was always plenty of work to do setting things up. James had been taken on as the summer help.

Emily had been nineteen years old, fresh out of sixth form and due to start at college in the autumn. She manned the refreshment kiosk for Benito and one day had served James with a cup of tea.

James had been everything a girl could wish for. Good looking, charming and fun to be with. His Scottish accent had been to die for and he had been forced to repeat his order for tea as Emily stared at him, speechless. The summer sun had lightened his sandy hair to a copper gold colour reminding Emily of a Greek god. He was quite simply perfect. Emily blushed now as she remembered how she had gaped at him.

There was a lively young set on the

scene that summer and Emily and James had taken to hanging around together. Emily had introduced James to the local crowd. Every night there were beach barbecues or parties, or a disco. Then one evening James and Emily found that due to a mix up over dates they were the only ones on the beach. They went for a moonlit walk and listened to the waves washing the sand and that was the night Emily had fallen in love with James Bradshaw.

A wry smile twisted Emily's lips. What had she known of love? James certainly hadn't loved her, despite all the sweet nothings he had whispered in her ear. When James had kissed her in the entrance to the old boathouse, Emily didn't think she had ever been happier in her life.

Later that week Emily found out the bitter truth. James had been two-timing her with Lucy Jackson. Lucy was standing in for her mother, the fortune-teller, Madame Zora, while she was away tending to a family crisis.

Emily and Lucy had been school friends, but they were never close. Lucy had had her eye on James ever since he appeared on the scene. The fact that she had a regular boyfriend made no difference to Lucy.

Emily believed James's story about a boys' night out until Lucy informed her with a knowing smirk that she and James had enjoyed a romantic evening, just the two of them, walking along the cliffs and if Lucy Jackson was to be believed, James had kissed her in the doorway of the old boathouse too and whispered the same sweet nothings in her ear.

Fired up with fury, Emily hadn't given herself a moment to think how foolishly she was behaving. She wanted revenge and she wanted it now. It had been easy to salvage some old plasterboard amongst Benito's recycling and there was always a ready supply of paints for the notices he used to put up advertising forthcoming attractions.

Emily had used the boldest, most

lurid, pink spray paint she could find. Her cheeks flamed with embarrassment as she remembered the spectacle of her artistic graffiti crudely displayed on six-foot high plasterboard strategically placed outside Madame Zora's fortune-telling caravan.

She couldn't remember the exact words she had used, but casual passers by were left in no doubt as to the nature of James Bradshaw's relationship with Lucy Jackson.

The ensuing uproar exceeded even Emily's expectations as she crouched behind the carousel and watched a furious Lucy Jackson try to rip the plasterboard to bits. Someone contacted the local paper and a freelance photographer was dispatched to the seafront to take Lucy's picture and it duly appeared emblazoned across the front page of that week's edition.

Benito, a family man of Italian descent, did not welcome complications of this nature and when he read the story, had fired James on the spot.

Lucy's boyfriend had asserted his manhood and promptly got engaged to her before she could cause any more trouble, and in order to escape the gossip Madame Zora had moved her fortune-telling caravan further down the coastline.

Looking back on things in a calmer frame of mind, Emily supposed she was lucky that no-one had taken the incident any further. They might have done had Lucy Jackson not made such a good job of destroying the evidence.

Suffused with guilt over her behaviour, Emily resigned from her job in the little kiosk, telling Benito she needed time to get ready for her new term at college and the next week she had left West Hampton to take up her place on her media studies course.

She hadn't actually signed her pink work of art, but she was pretty sure both Lucy and James would have suspected who was responsible for the artistic display.

A reluctant smile curved Emily's lips.

She'd heard a rumour on the grapevine that James had been furious when Benito had fired him and demanded to be allowed to give his side of the story, but James, it seemed, had broken more than the average number of female hearts during his short summer stay in West Hampton, including that of Benito's niece and Benito had not given him the time of day.

And now James Bradshaw was back.

Emily reached the harbour. She sat down on the sea wall and watched some children building a sand castle. The scene was so peaceful and family friendly. That was exactly how Emily wanted West Hampton to remain. She wasn't against progress, but if James Bradshaw had ideas of turning The Little Alhambra into a garish cinema with flashing neon lights and crude pinball machines, then he would have a fight on his hands.

Emily was older now, and a few years wiser than the impressionable young girl who had fallen for his Scottish charm. James Bradshaw would soon discover Emily Sinclair could still fight her corner and these days her methods were a lot more professional than those she used on Lucy Jackson.

A Face from The Past Returns

The stage was decorated with streamers and balloons and dangling Chinese lanterns bobbed about in the wings, casting vivid swathes of emerald green, vermilion and amethyst over the props. Ted had gone totally over the top. Every bit of party scenery he could lay his hands on in the storeroom had been wheeled onto the stage ready to be used for Joe's leaving party.

The tables were groaning with food. Betty from the bakery had done them proud with a huge cake iced in the shape of The Little Alhambra. It was decorated with more candles than was probably tactful, but no-one was counting.

A plentiful supply of liquid refreshment was on hand to cool throats that

Emily knew from past experience would be parched from too much networking in loud voices with old friends.

Joe was a much loved member of the community and word had soon got round West Hampton and the theatrical circles that The Little Alhambra had been sold and Joe was retiring to spend more time with his family.

For the past two-and-a-half weeks, Emily's life had been a frantic round of contacting old colleagues, updating them on the news and swearing them to secrecy before inviting them to the party she was arranging for Joe. It was an impossible task. The theatre folk Joe and Emily mixed with were incapable of keeping anything quiet for longer than two minutes and soon the airwaves were buzzing with the news and Joe had discovered what was going on.

'You don't have to do this,' he protested but he didn't make a very good pretence of voicing his objection to Emily. She could tell from his heightened colour and happy smile that he was looking forward to the party as much as she was, but was too embarrassed to admit it.

Ever since her parents had sold up their bed and breakfast business and moved to Minorca, Joe and his wife had taken Emily under their wing. She had been included in all their celebrations and made to feel an extended part of the family.

'I want to, Joe,' she insisted. 'It's payback time for all the lovely parties you've given me, besides you didn't think we'd let you go without a proper send off did you? What do you take us for?'

Behind his rimless glasses, Joe's smile was definitely on the shaky side.

'I love this business, Emily, you know that and if circumstances hadn't forced me to sell up, I'd be alongside you fighting tooth and nail for our survival.'

'I know that, Joe,' she assured him, 'and there's no need to worry about us. The Little Alhambra will survive. James

Bradshaw won't know what's hit him if he starts any funny business.'

'If I hadn't had you to take over the reins,' Joe insisted, 'I might not have considered retirement, but I know you're the right person and the old place needs an injection of young blood. A word of advice though, Emily, James Bradshaw is an astute business-man. Don't dismiss his suggestions out of hand. Think them through first.'

Emily nodded, not wanting to dis-agree with Joe, but very much doubting she would take that bit of advice on board.

'Have you heard from him, James Bradshaw?' she asked as they shared their afternoon mug of tea in Joe's cubbyhole of an office.

Joe shook his head. 'His agent tells me he's bought one of those studio flats that overlook the bay and that he'll be moving in shortly.'

'Harley's Point?'

A shadow passed over Joe's face. Harley's Point had been the source of much local controversy. Until two years ago it had been a rather rundown and neglected area of the seafront, then on the back of an article in one of the glossy magazines, extolling the virtues of West Hampton, a developer had upgraded the old buildings and converted them into executive properties for the new breed of professionals eager to have a weekend base where they could entertain their guests on the south coast.

To his credit, the developer had retained the frontage of the old Victorian warehouse and wherever possible, used original sourced materials for the building work. The Council had been impressed with the standard and professionalism of the project and given it their full backing and approval.

All the same, there was still a hard core of opposition to the scheme and the locals treated anyone occupying the new studios with a certain amount of mistrust.

'We mustn't let old prejudices stand

in the way of development,' Joe said, rather half-heartedly.

'You're right,' Emily agreed. 'Now is not the time to bring up that old chestnut, it's a done deal and there's nothing we can do about it, besides which,' she drained the last of her coffee, 'I've got a party to organise. Be there,' she added as a parting shot to Joe.

'You aren't going to spray my past misdemeanours all over the stage in pink graffiti are you?' There was a twinkle in his eye as he added in the face of Emily's embarrassment. 'Worse kept secret in West Hampton that bit of nonsense was, apart from the plans for my party,' he added.

'I don't know what you're talking about.' Emily did her best to make a dignified exit, but when you were petite and relied on the highest of heels to give you stature, it wasn't easy.

Joe's laughter rang in her ears as she stumbled down the corridor hoping against hope he wouldn't make that story a part of his farewell speech.

She should have guessed her misdemeanour would be outed and like all good stories over the years the details had been embellished. Would time have healed James Bradshaw's pride? Or would he still hold a grudge?

★   ★   ★

On the night of the party guests began pouring into the theatre from seven o'clock onwards. Emily had posted the final details on the theatre website and all day her in box had bulged with e-mails and promises to attend. Due to the nature of their work, many of Joe's contacts weren't sure they would be free until the last moment, but judging by the turnout it looked as though the affair was going to be a roaring success.

Car after car blocked the side roads as people searched frantically for parking spaces. The sound of booming voices more used to being exercised on stage floated up from the seafront where an emergency car park had been opened by a quick thinking chef, whose restaurant was closed for the evening.

Space was already at a premium in the theatre stalls and several guests drifted into the ornamental garden that had originally been designed by The Little Alhambra's Victorian entrepreneur. Indian artefacts jostled for space in the Chinese water garden creating a colourful mix of ethnic cultures.

Ted had again come up trumps with some night lights he had discovered stowed away in yet another corner of the storeroom and although the late April evening was mild and the light had not yet faded from the day the ornamental garden benefited from the soft glow of warmth they created.

Emily strolled under the trees catching up with old friends just as Lottie and Orlando's three-litre Bentley purred its way into their designated parking bay under the oak tree.

As usual their arrival created more than a stir of interest. Lottie and

Orlando had been major players of both stage and screen in their day, and even though their star had now faded, neither of them had let retirement slow them down.

They lived in a comfortable farmhouse style property on the outskirts of West Hampton and both were extremely active on the local scene and staunch patrons of first nights at The Little Alhambra.

Orlando, dapper in dinner dress and trademark Panama hat that he always wore winter and summer alike, leapt out of the driving seat and strode round to the passenger side to where a regal Lottie was waiting for him to open the passenger door.

Lottie was very proud of her legs, a legacy of her dancing days, and tonight she wore the sheerest of tights to show off her still shapely ankles. Her dress was of orange swirly silk; full skirted and tight waisted, it provided a vibrant contrast to the purple bolero that graced her elegant shoulders.

'See Dame Lottie is making her usual entrance stage right,' one of the party guests gumshoed out of the corner of her mouth, then quickly smothered her amusement as Lottie, hearing her nickname, sent a withering look in the direction of the unfortunate party guest.

Lottie had added a feathery pink fascinator to the ensemble and it sat atop her snow-white hair, fixed at a very jaunty angle. Her violet eyes widened with delight at the sea of faces on the forecourt of The Little Alhambra. They were all looking in her direction and there was nothing Lottie adored more than being the centre of attention.

'Hello, everyone.'

Her voice was low and smoky and despite her advanced years still had every male present, young and old alike, longing to be her slave.

'Darling.'

She opened her arms wide and the next moment Emily was smothered in a waft of the exclusive perfume Lottie once told her had been especially created for her by one of her French gentlemen friends.

'You look absolutely wonderful.'

In her functional scarlet wrap-over dress Emily knew she was absolutely no competition for the glamorous Lottie, but when your self confidence was having a bit of an identity crisis, as Emily's was now, it was nice to be told you looked wonderful.

Underneath the sophisticated veneer, Lottie had a kind and generous heart and Emily happily succumbed to her embrace.

'Dear girl, absolutely splendid show. Enjoying myself thoroughly.'

Orlando's moustache tickled Emily on the cheek as he kissed her.

'Don't talk so daft.' Lottie's native Yorkshire accent was always more pronounced when she was off duty and relaxed. 'You've only just arrived. You haven't had a chance to get going.'

Orlando raised his bushy eyebrows in amused tolerance. Bickering was a way of life to him and Lottie, but it didn't lessen the deep affection they held for each other.

'So, old Joe's off to eat hay, is he?' Orlando asked. 'Not before time.'

'He's younger than you, Orlando Fawcett,' Lottie pointed out. 'What's all this about James Bradshaw?' she quizzed Emily. 'I've heard so many rumours I don't know which one to believe.'

'Joe's sold out to him.'

'So it's true?' Lottie looked scandalised.

'It was either that or close the place down,' Emily replied.

'Well, if he gets up to any of his old tricks, let me know.' Lottie nodded, 'and don't pretend you don't know what I'm talking about. He was the one who broke your heart, wasn't he?'

'My heart wasn't broken,' Emily insisted. She could feel hot colour staining her cheeks. Lottie didn't have the quietest of voices and several people were looking with interest in their direction.

Lottie raised a disbelieving eyebrow. 'And I'm a shrinking violet. Now, don't forget, darling, my word is as good as my bond. Just let me near him if there's any nonsense. I'll show him he can't mistreat my girl and get away with it.'

'I can't really talk about it now,' Emily tried to dismiss James Bradshaw from Lottie's mindset before she did anything foolish.

'Quite right,' Orlando agreed, 'don't want to spoil the party atmosphere, do we?'

'Well, if you need any power to your elbow,' Lottie patted Emily's arm, 'you know where to come. Now I am off to make the acquaintance of that adorable young man in the turquoise shirt. Doesn't he have eyelashes to die for? I am so jealous.'

Leaving Orlando to deal with the dispensing of the generous supply of champagne they always brought with them, Lottie drifted towards the action in a haze of French perfume. Emily, deciding to check on the last minute presentation details headed indoors towards the stage.

Now the moment was here, she hadn't expected to feel quite so emotional over Joe's departure even though she'd had more than two weeks to get used to the idea that he was handing over the reins to a younger man. There had been no word from James Bradshaw since Joe had gone public and Emily still had no idea whether or not she would have a job in a week's time.

James Bradshaw ran an efficient portfolio of properties. Would he want to make a Victorian playhouse part of that portfolio? The theatre paid its way in the summer months and the pantomime was always a sell out. All the same, the over all profits did not make encouraging reading. The Alhambra was in urgent need of cosmetic repair and James Bradshaw would have no sentimental attachment to the place.

Emily straightened her shoulders and flipped back her neat bob of chestnut hair. Negative thinking had never been her style. She was more than up to the challenge of facing James Bradshaw and had already started work on a business plan to put before him.

'All set for the presentation?' Ted hissed in her ear, making her jump.

'Yes, of course,' Emily replied.

'Best start getting everyone in then,' he hinted, 'Orlando is getting carried away serving champagne from the boot of that car of his and you know how generous he can be. If we don't get things moving soon, there won't be any presentation.'

Ted's advice galvanised Emily into action. Quite how they managed it, Emily didn't know, but within fifteen minutes the stalls were crammed with guests, still busily catching up on gossip and clutching Orlando's champagne flutes. The lucky ones settled down in the plush red velvet and gold seats. The rest jostled for space at the back of the theatre and began a slow handclap, the sound interrupted only by cheers and the popping of champagne corks from Lottie and Orlando's private box at the front of the stage.

Gripping her microphone and quelling any last minute nerves, Emily strode onto the stage to a chorus of cheering from the rowdier element of the guests. Dazzled by the footlights, it took her a few moments to quieten things down.

Joe was already seated in a prop armchair; Maisie resplendent in the prettiest of oatmeal lace dresses was seated in a matching one by his side. They were holding hands and smiling tenderly at each other. For a moment Emily faltered in her stride. They had been married for so many years and looked so happy together she felt positively jealous. Behind them stood an assortment of children and grand-children, all beaming with pride. Emily wondered briefly if she would ever find a love like that.

Emily cleared her throat and began her speech.

'Welcome to The Little Alhambra,

everyone. It's lovely to see so many old faces and new ones.' She smiled at Joe's youngest grandchild, asleep in his mother's arms. 'I promise to keep it short but I'm so glad you could all join us today to pay tribute to Joe and Maisie Sykes.' A spontaneous bout of applause broke out. 'Over the years Joe, with Maisie's unstinting support, has built up the reputation of The Little Alhambra sometimes in the face of considerable conflict, but he always came through.'

'Despite bossy management.' An enthusiastic bout of applause greeted the throwaway remark.

'Although I know at times Joe has been a bit of a hard taskmaster,' a groan now ran through the audience as Emily battled on with her speech, 'we don't know how we're going to manage without him.'

'Hear, hear.'

The applause and cheers that greeted her words was deafening.

Emily then recounted one or two of

the more humorous anecdotes that had gone down in The Alhambra's legend, before inviting everyone to raise their glasses in a toast to Joe and Maisie.

'May your ghost light never go out,' Emily said, referring to the superstition of keeping the stage illuminated when it was not in use, in order to ward off malevolent spirits.

'Break a leg,' several members of the audience chimed in.

A commotion from the wings preceded Ted's arrival as he staggered onto the stage with two huge striped deckchairs decorated with streamers and party bows. He presented them to Joe and Maisie amid more applause and enthusiastic whistling.

Joe rose to his feet. 'Thank you very much, everybody. Maisie and I will enjoy using them once we've worked out how to operate the mechanism. Nothing so dangerous as a deckchair,' he quipped then turned to look at Emily. 'As Emily well knows, and what an appropriate parting gift,' he winked at her. 'Some of you may remember a certain James Bradshaw who spent a summer down here on the seafront, as a deckchair attendant.'

'Got your pink aerosol at the ready, Emily?' a wit called out from the back row. 'Perhaps you'd like to keep your hand in with a little light decorating in case things get a bit sticky with the new owner?'

Emily knew her complexion was almost as red as her dress. Would that wretched story never die? She plastered a smile on her face, not wanting to be taken for a bad sport as everyone exploded into happy laughter.

As if on cue there was a further disturbance at the back of the theatre. A hush now fell on the exuberant audience as the new arrival emerged from behind the curtains and began to make his way slowly down the centre aisle to the stage.

It had been six years since Emily had seen James Bradshaw. She gulped. The years had treated him well. Today he had replaced the white T shirt and shorts he'd always worn on the beach for tailored chinos and designer polo shirt.

The eyes were deeper blue than Emily remembered and still had the power to make her heart flutter. Annoyed with her reaction at seeing James Bradshaw again, Emily made the briefest acknowledgement to his gesture of greeting.

'Allow me.' James turned his attention to a struggling Maisie and with a charming smile gallantly relieved her of her deckchair and to a round of applause, erected it correctly and placed it before her.

'Thank you very much,' she gushed as he guided her into it, 'how kind.'

'Not at all. As you can see,' his next remark was addressed to Emily, 'I haven't entirely forgotten the skills I acquired from my summer's stay in West Hampton. In fact,' he added to the audience at large, 'I haven't forgotten anything about that summer and I've hated the colour pink ever since.'

The audience erupted into whoops of delight. A chorus of *For He's A Jolly Good Fellow* drowned the laughter that greeted this interchange, as Joe attempted to blow out all the candles on his cake.

Emily did her best to melt away from the happy scene, but before she could make good her exit James put out a hand to detain her and she was forced to stand hand in hand with him as the singing continued.

'Weren't thinking of leaving just yet, were you?' James murmured in her ear.

'I've got a lot to do, I . . . '

'Nothing that won't wait,' James insisted, 'and it's important we present a united front, wouldn't you say? We don't want any more rumours about our relationship flying around do we?'

'We don't have one,' Emily hissed.

'Yes we do. I'm your new boss.'

'That isn't what I meant.' Emily knew her complexion must resemble an over ripe beetroot. Luckily most of the partygoers were enjoying themselves too much to notice what was happening between them on stage.

'Isn't it? Then why don't you tell me what you did mean?' The smile James delivered was nowhere near as charming as the one he had used on Maisie. Despite the heat in the theatre it made Emily want to shiver.

'I was referring to a personal relationship, not a professional one.'

'Now, there I do agree with you.'

'You do?' Emily couldn't disguise her surprise.

'Our new relationship is purely professional and in my capacity as owner of the theatre, what I say goes, wouldn't you agree?'

'Yes, of course.'

'So glad we understand each other. Now I suggest you smile at me the way you used to six years ago before you rubbished my reputation.'

'That's taking professionalism too far,' Emily retaliated.

'Please yourself.' James didn't look in the least put out by her objection, 'but The Herald photographer is standing behind you waiting to take our picture. Do you really want your scowling face plastered all over next week's front page?'

'What?'

Emily spun round as a flash bulb went off in her face.

'First round to me I would think, wouldn't you?' James whispered in her ear.

'These yourself' 'imoraloti' lootilii
die-first-you out. By not brunchon. But
the Herald photographer is amazing
beautiful was eneira to take our picture
Do you realize the vulue of a June the
to....

'I'm An Actor, Currently Resting'

Tricia Longfellow sipped her soft drink
as she watched Toby French work the
bar. It had been an exhausting morning
presenting the phone-in from the
country club and she needed to take
time out to unwind. She had been
monitoring the calls before they were
given air time to make sure the caller
wasn't a crank on a personal agenda.
Listener participation had been encouraging and very vibrant but Tricia wasn't
sure if the broadcast had gone that well.
Somewhere along the line she felt it had
failed to hit the right note.

This had been her first chance at
helping out with an outside broadcast
and she had hoped for a more
groundbreaking window airing new
ideas.

There was a lot happening at the current time in West Hampton. The purchase of The Little Alhambra by James Bradshaw had received significant media attention and a celebrity chef had expressed interest in a local property with a view to opening a prestigious new restaurant. Tricia was eager to place West Hampton on the map, but she felt today's programme missed the mark. Her grey eyes narrowed thoughtfully.

'Toby, isn't it?' she peered at the barman's gold name badge discreetly edged in green.

'Yes, madam.'

His voice was polite and betrayed his college education. There were a lot of 'Tobys' doing holiday jobs in the area, although he looked a little old to be a student, more likely filling in while he was job hunting, Tricia thought.

'So, Toby, Tricia Longfellow,' she introduced herself. 'What did you think of the show?' Tricia made sure the natural light shining through the large double windows caught her at her best angle. Her uncle had taught her the importance of presentation and Tricia sensed someone like Toby could be useful to her. He was representative of the generation of listener her radio station wanted to attract.

With a charisma that sat easily on his strong shoulders, Tricia had seen the effect his effortless charm had on the patrons of the country club, particularly the female ones. Throughout the broadcast he had been on hand, serving drinks and answering any queries that arose during the course of the morning. He wore his crinkly mid brown hair slightly too long and his eyes were a little too close together for conventional good looks, but in spite of these short comings Toby looked good and Tricia could understand why he had been picked as the country club's front man for the occasion.

A local advertiser had sponsored the joint radio station and country club promotion. The programme controller had detailed Tricia to help out and although she had kept her doubts about the style of the promotion to herself, she felt these doubts had been reflected in what could only be described as a disappointing broadcast.

There had been no conflict between the patrons of the club and the listeners phoning in. Most of the country club clientele were grandparents and understood the problems and pressures of modern life and the younger generation had respected their wisdom and experience, which had resulted in a less than stimulating phone-in.

Tricia suspected that on air interviews with some of the incomers from Harley's Point would make much more stimulating listening. She knew from personal experience that local feelings ran high on that one, but before she put her proposal to the controller she needed to listen to as many personal views as possible, and Toby was the sort of person she needed to make a valuable input to her project.

'You want my opinion on today's presentation?' Toby finished wiping down the counter. He placed the damp cloth over the taps to dry.

'Everyone's opinion is important to us,' Tricia's quoted the station's mission statement.

'Well,' Toby took a deep breath, 'it's a great idea from the advertiser's point of view, but you went about it the wrong way.'

Tricia stiffened. This was not what she had been expecting. 'Excuse me?'

Toby gave her the full benefit of his lazy smile.

'You did ask for my opinion,' he reminded her. 'I thought you wanted an honest viewpoint, but if you're not used to constructive criticism then yes, it was a great programme.'

He turned away from her to speak to a customer. Tricia sipped her fruit juice as she thought things through. Her fingertips tingled in anticipation. She was right. This could be the opportunity she was looking for. Due to family influence

Tricia had been offered the job of production assistant and she knew her appointment had created a certain amount of resentment among her colleagues.

She needed to prove she was up to the job and not just a puppet placement on behalf of her uncle, although at the same time what she did not want was to get herself a reputation as a trouble-maker.

So far Tricia had played along with the bosses and not rocked the boat, but the benefits of Toby's feedback would be interesting, even if, for the moment, she kept them to herself.

'Go on, I'm listening,' she prompted Toby as he finished with his customer.

'This confrontation thing,' he began.

'Yes?'

'Two groups of people from different walks of life thrown together for half an hour or so doesn't always work. Today's guests turned the programme into a cosy fireside chat. They all agreed with each other. Where's the stimulation in that?'

'All right,' Tricia used the full benefit of her burgeoning interviewing technique on Toby. 'What would you suggest?'

'What you need is a focus on the modern positive aspect of life in West Hampton. Throw different people together by all means, but make them interesting.'

'Are you saying the country club clientele are dull?'

Toby raised his eyebrows theatrically and Tricia flushed. That remark had been a step too far.

'I didn't say that, you did.' Toby spoke softly as if addressing a recalcitrant child.

'What I meant was,' Tricia looked hastily over her shoulder hoping she hadn't been overheard, before leaning forward and lowering her voice she asked, 'what have you got in mind?'

'Me?' The blue eyes widened. 'Nothing at all. I'm the temporary barman here.'

Tricia tapped a manicured nail on her long slim glass of fruit juice.

'Want another?' Toby asked.

She tucked a stray strand of her newly highlighted hair behind her ear.

'Please,' she smiled, 'then why don't you tell me about yourself?'

Most people loved talking about themselves. As a ploy it usually worked and Toby French proved to be no exception to the rule.

'I'm due for my break now. We could sit on the terrace. It's always quiet at this time of day.'

Tricia strolled outside into the sunshine, her dress showing off her figure to its full advantage. She spent a lot of her allowance on her appearance.

Although she was grateful to her uncle for his help, she did not want to have to rely on him to always be there to support her career. She wanted to be a name in her own right. Tricia's degree in media and journalism would not open many doors unless she went the extra mile and for that Tricia knew she had to make the most of her opportunities.

'So, Toby,' Tricia smiled as they settled down opposite each other. 'You're not really a barman, are you?'

'Actually I'm an actor, currently resting,' he delivered his reply with his trademark deprecating smile.

That explained the casual self-assurance Tricia thought as Toby asked, 'You don't happen to know a good agent, do you?'

''Fraid not.' She shook her head.

'Pity.'

Tricia relaxed in the sunshine. She should have guessed about Toby. Like most members of his profession, Toby was constantly playing a part. At the moment he was acting the barman.

'You're looking for work?'

'I was offered the lead in the new production scheduled at The Little Alhambra, but it fell through.'

'Because of James Bradshaw?' Tricia asked.

Like everyone else in West Hampton she had talked of nothing else since the news had been announced that he was to be the new owner of The Little Alhambra. She had hoped for a press release or some extra information about James Bradshaw that would enable her to learn more about him, but he was notoriously reclusive when it came to his private life. Apart from one press announcement no further bulletins had been issued.

An exclusive interview with James Bradshaw would be exactly the vehicle to further Tricia's career.

'The Alhambra was sold the week before a new production was scheduled,' Toby explained. 'Emily, she's the manager there, was very nice about it, but she explained they needed to close the theatre while things were sorted out. We were the unlucky ones. Our play was the first production to suffer. We may get a rebooking later in the season, but no one's making any promises and for the moment things have been put on hold.' Toby shrugged. 'Story of my life.'

'There wasn't another theatre you could use?'

'Most productions are run on a shoestring and ours was no exception. The backers pulled out when The Alhambra cancelled.'

'I'm sorry,' Tricia sympathised.

'So as I had nothing else booked I decided to make the best of it and spend the summer down here. I suppose I thought I might be able to get a part in another play if someone falls out for any reason. I've left my details with The Little Alhambra but so far I've heard nothing. Still it's early days.'

'What do you do when you're resting?'

'When the weather's fine I hang around the seafront. A friend of mine runs the water sports centre and I pick up the occasional day's work, helping with the water ski-ing, fishing, diving, that sort of thing. The season is beginning to look up and the weekends are quite busy. It's as good a way as any to earn a living.'

'And you think local radio should interview some of these weekenders?'

'Only a suggestion,' Toby smiled. 'I know they bring in a lot of business but that's not to say they are popular with the residents.

'I agree,' Tricia hesitated.

'So what's stopping you?' Toby looked at her expectantly.

'Office politics. I'm the new girl.'

'And it doesn't do to make waves?'

'Something like that,' Tricia agreed.

Toby had removed his jacket displaying the country club logo and easing down the knot in his green tie, had undone the top buttons of his shirt. Tricia could see suntanned flesh that bore evidence of his outdoor life.

'Are you from round here?' she asked him.

He shook his head. 'I'm from the Midlands, one of the most landlocked parts of the country. Think that's why I like the sea.'

'Do you live at the club?'

Toby hesitated. 'No,' he replied eventually, 'I've got family in the area.'

'And you stay with them?'

'My aunt and her husband live just outside West Hampton. I have the run of their studio and I come and go more or less as I please.'

Toby's body language alerted Tricia's journalistic instinct. There was something he wasn't telling her.

'That's very convenient,' she smiled encouragingly, 'an aunt with a studio?'

'Where do you live?' Toby asked, ignoring the question in her voice.

'I, er,' Tricia cleared her throat. It was her turn to feel uneasy. 'I've got a small open plan apartment in the new seafront development.'

'Harley's Point?'

'It's not something I often admit to,' Tricia said.

Although she was local born and bred she had been the victim of some mild unpleasantness, chiefly from her colleagues when they discovered where she lived.

Toby whistled under his breath. 'I'm impressed.'

'It's my uncle's actually, but like you

with your studio, I have free use of it.'

'Then you'll know James Bradshaw.'

'I've never met him.'

'He's your neighbour.'

'What?' Tricia snapped to attention.

'James Bradshaw's got the penthouse suite.'

'How do you know?' Tricia demanded, annoyed that she had not discovered this useful piece of news herself.

'My aunt told me.'

'Is your aunt a reliable source?' Tricia asked.

'Toby?' The manager called over interrupting them, waving his watch in the air and pointing towards the time.

'Coming,' he replied. 'Sorry, got to go. I'm needed in the restaurant.' He stood up. 'Nice meeting you, Tricia.' He shook her hand. 'Any time you fancy a spot of water ski-ing you know where to find me.'

Emily And James Must
Work Together

'You don't understand.' Emily wished James wouldn't look at her quite so intently. His deep blue eyes were as distracting now as they had been six years ago. Reminding herself it was important to focus, Emily pressed on with her presentation. 'The Little Alhambra isn't only a theatre it is an institution.'

'I am well aware of that,' James clipped back at her, 'but institutions don't last forever and my feeling is that this one has had its day.'

'No.' Emily leaned forward. 'How can you say that?'

'It happens to be my opinion.' There was a slight softening of his lips. 'But if you disagree, state your case. Make me change my mind.'

Emily cleared her throat well aware that James was putting her on the spot. He had a lot to learn if he thought she was the same girl he had so cruelly deceived in the past. She flashed him her most professional smile to show his attitude didn't faze her. Even though her head was buzzing she was enjoying the challenge of confrontation. Meetings with Joe were cosy affairs. This meeting was anything but.

'The theatre survived wartime bombing, floods, a lightning strike and the great storm of the eighties. Hardly a tree was left standing in West Hampton but the voluntary services used our facilities to set up a soup kitchen. People came from miles around. It was one of the main liaison points of the area. I believe closing down the theatre would rip the heart out of the community.'

'Be that as it may,' James began.

'I haven't finished,' Emily insisted.

James raised his eyebrows in surprise. The office at the back of the theatre was not the best place to hold their first business meeting. Cramped spacing meant she was sitting far too close to him for comfort.

It had been a week since Joe's retirement party. James had only stayed a brief half hour after the photo shoot before being called away on an urgent matter, but his guest appearance had left Emily in no doubt of her position. James had not forgotten or forgiven her.

He was well aware who was responsible for the pink graffiti sprayed on cardboard outside Madame Zora's caravan and he intended to get his revenge by closing down the theatre.

During one of the most uncomfortable half hours of her life he had forced Emily to stand beside him on the stage and smile as a stream of guests crowded around Joe and Maisie all offering their good wishes for his retirement.

When she tried to let go of his hand, James increased the pressure of his fingers entwining his with hers. Short of engaging in an undignified tussle, there was little Emily could do. To her surprise James greeted Ivy and Ted by their first names and complimented Ivy on all the hard work she had done to make the party a success. A beaming Ivy sung James's praise later and suggested that perhaps they had all been wrong about him.

'Such a pleasant man,' she cooed to Ted, 'I can't believe all those stories about him being ruthless.'

Emily could. Before James left the party he had asked her for an in depth spreadsheet into the theatre's financial structure.

After a week of intense paperwork and research and sleepless nights, Emily's facts and figures were now on the desk in front of James. He afforded them no more than a cursory glance before informing her of his decision.

'I can't afford to be sentimental about a theatre, neither am I a charity. The Alhambra is situated on two acres of prime development site and it's not making a profit. It's barely breaking even.'

'But if you had bothered to read my report, properly,' Emily was pleased her words caused a flash of discomfort to cross James's face, 'you'll see that with good investment The Alhambra won't be a lost cause.'

'I disagree with you.'

'I'm sure I could turn the situation around if you give me the chance.'

'You think so?' James looked unconvinced.

'I do.'

'So what you are saying is that Joe, with his immense experience and contacts in the theatre world, wasn't up to the job?'

'No.' Emily bit her lip, not wanting to be disloyal to her erstwhile boss. 'That's not what I'm saying at all.' She ran a hand through her hair, unaware her felt tip pen left a blue streak on her forehead.

James's expression softened a fraction as he looked at the ink stain. He leaned back in his chair and after a short pause said, 'Go on then. I'm listening. The floor is yours. You've got five minutes to pitch me a line.'

Emily took another deep breath to steady her rapid heartbeat. She couldn't afford to get things wrong and the next five minutes could possibly change her entire life forever.

'Joe was tired. His health was poor and after a bad bout of 'flu last winter Maisie began persuading him to retire. She can be quite a formidable lady when the mood is on her and as the months went by she upped the pressure. With all that on his mind, I think Joe missed several good marketing opportunities.'

'Such as?' James clipped back at her.

'We could introduce a loyalty voucher scheme and promotions to coincide with local events. That would provide free advertising. We could make the theatre available for television and film work. It has a very individual frontage and I've already made enquiries and had some interested feedback. Local people would be more than willing to act as extras, so it would provide a source of employment as well.'

James raised his eyebrows. 'Film work?' he repeated, hardly bothering to disguise his disbelief.

'The Little Alhambra is tailor-made for it. It's got position, atmosphere and style. It's perfect for period dramas. It's not too big and we don't have a huge great board of directors to get in the way of any negotiations, so what's not to like about the idea?'

'You've got another couple of minutes to go,' James reminded her.

'West Hampton has good transport connections, road and rail, a big choice of hotels and cheaper boarding houses and those new restaurants on the seafront have put us on the map. We have featured in the Sunday supplements. The surrounding scenery is stunning, all of which makes for good marketing.

'West Hampton is fast growing into a

fashionable weekend and holiday resort, all factors that would bring added custom to the theatre. There would be no staffing problems. I have a list of willing part-timers who could step in at a moment's notice to help out. I've also got a drawer full of celebrity endorsements, I'm sure we could persuade a big name to front any promotion.'

Emily leaned forward, her eyes earnest with enthusiasm as she waited for James's take on her proposal.

'It all sounds very impressive, but I'm still not convinced.' James's eyes clashed into hers. 'The sort of projects you have in mind would need months to show any real financial turn around. Quite frankly I don't think you have the resources to carry it through. My decision to close still stands.'

'This is because of us, isn't it?' Emily's usually cool hazel eyes narrowed in thinly veiled anger.

She hadn't meant to lose control so early on in the meeting, but being with James again it was as though the years had rolled away. He was treating her like the young inexperienced adolescent she had been, hopelessly in love with him as she served teas and snacks to the holidaymakers.

'What exactly do you mean?' The tone of James's voice gave nothing away.

'You know perfectly well what I mean,' Emily retaliated.

'You're going to have to refresh my memory.' The suggestion of amusement tweaked the corner of James's mouth.

Emily blinked. He'd backed her neatly into a corner and there was no way she could get out of it unless she admitted to being responsible for spraying pink graffiti all over the seafront, something she had never done.

'Nothing to say?' he teased, 'then let me help you. Could it be you're referring to the very regrettable incident involving a can of spray paint?' James's lips continued to twitch as he looked at her, 'because if you are, then please don't flatter yourself. I base my business decisions on much higher criteria than the foolish behaviour of,' he paused before adding, 'an anonymous artist.'

Emily squirmed in her seat. Like everyone else in West Hampton, he knew exactly who the anonymous artist had been. Emily was beginning to wonder why she hadn't signed her piece of artwork and have done with it. The incident had been so out of character and one she had never repeated, yet it had come back to haunt her time and again.

It was nothing more than a moment's madness when for a split second in time she had thought she was in love with James Bradshaw. Looking at him now, smiling in that superior way of his, she knew she must have been mad to imagine entertaining any emotion for such a man.

'So what you're saying is you're prepared to destroy the livelihood of a significant part of a hard working community because we're not making enough money to line your pocket?'

It was a below the belt remark but Emily was goaded beyond endurance. So many people depended on The Little Alhambra for work. At Joe's party she had received many pledges of support, a lot of it voluntary and she had promised to do everything in her power to persuade James to keep the theatre open, but she had failed at the first fence because James Bradshaw had turned into a selfish man who had lost all traces of humanity and could see no further than the next deal.

An angry flush stained the base of James's neck. Emily tossed back her head pleased her angry barb had found its target. If this was going to be her Joan of Arc moment then she intended it to be an honourable one.

'Would it change your mind if I tendered my resignation?'

'What possible use would your resignation be to anyone?' James snapped back.

'I thought perhaps you could try running the theatre yourself, or put in a manager of your own choice.' Emily couldn't resist adding, 'one who doesn't have a sordid past. Then after six months, a year say, if things haven't changed, you could close the theatre down with a clear conscience and let someone build a horrible entertainment megaplex on the site. It's your decision.'

If this was what it was like to play poker then Emily was glad she had never learned the rules of the game. She had called James's bluff. Would he take up her challenge?

'That's your take on the situation — six months' reprieve?'

'Yes. Can't you see, James, I mean Mr Bradshaw, no-one will blame you for failing if you at least try? Please?' she added in a half whisper. 'You can't let West Hampton down.'

James looked down at the table, his fingers fumbling with the corners of her printed report.

'Very well,' he nodded.

'You agree?' Emily's voice bordered alarmingly close to a screech as a surge of adrenaline coursed through her veins.

'We'll compromise. Nine months. That should allow for the Christmas pantomime profits to be included in the equation.'

'Yes!' Forgetting to whom she was talking, Emily power saluted her victory and beamed from ear to ear. At the cost of her own job security, she had won the day. 'You won't regret your decision. They're a great team. Ivy thinks you're wonderful. She'll do anything for you.'

'I'm very pleased to hear it.' Amusement again tugged the corner of James's mouth.

'Then of course there are all the kids from the college. We use them in the holidays. You know, selling ice creams and programmes and doing the tea trays for the seniors. They're a high-spirited bunch and not above playing a practical joke or two, so it's as well to have your wits about you when you're dealing with them, but they are great youngsters and very willing. I've got a note of all their details.'

'If I could just get a word in edgewise?' James enquired mildly.

'What? Oh, yes, of course. Sorry. Got a bit carried away. I love the old place you see. She won't let you down. I always imagine that The Alhambra is female. I see her as a rather grand lady, silly isn't it?'

'There will of course be certain conditions and a legal contract to be signed.'

'Well, let me be the first to say break a leg. By the way, theatre folk are a suspicious lot so don't start whistling backstage or mentioning the Scottish play or they'll be down on you like a ton of bricks.'

'Where are you going?' James demanded with a frown.

'I'm going home. I'm going to get out of this suit and then I'm going for a long walk along the cliff tops. I've spent every moment of the last week chained to a computer screen and I need to clear my head.'

'But I haven't finished outlining my proposal.'

'Then the sooner you appoint a new manager, the sooner you can get on with things. I could suggest a few suitable names, people who would be interested in the position.'

'Don't you want the job?'

'Me?' Emily stuttered. Her throat threatened to lock up completely as she tried to speak. 'You mean you want me to continue here as manager?'

'Didn't I just say that?' It was James's turn to look perplexed. 'That was quite some speech you made, almost had me cheering from the aisles.'

'But I thought . . . ' Emily ran out of words.

'You thought what exactly?'

'M . . . my resignation, I thought you'd accepted it.'

'Then you can think again, Ms Sinclair.'

'You mean you want me to see the project through?' Emily began to feel rather faint in the enclosed confines of the stuffy office.

'If you're not in on the deal, then it's off,' James said firmly. 'Those are my conditions. Take them or leave them. Do you accept my offer?'

'If you're sure?' Emily hesitated, still not certain she had heard him correctly.

'I'm sure, as long as you don't give me cause to regret my decision.'

'You won't,' Emily enthused, 'I mean I won't.'

James looked as though he wanted to say more but after a moment he lowered his eyes and returned his attention to Emily's report.

'Good, I shall give your appraisal my full attention over the weekend. Now this is what I've got in mind,' James looked up and frowned at her. 'Have I got a mark on the end of my nose or something?' he demanded.

'No.'

'Then why are you looking at me like that?'

'I,' Emily cleared her throat uncomfortably unaware that she had been close to throwing her arms around James's neck to thank him. 'I didn't think you'd want me on board the new set up, that's all.'

'Why? Are there more flaws in your character apart from the urge to paint al fresco?' A dimple dented his cheek.

'I . . . I . . . '

'Because if there are I'd like to know about them now.'

'N . . . no, there's nothing,' Emily stammered. She did her best to sound businesslike but it wasn't easy when she remembered the thrust of the tirade she had painted on Benito's tatty piece of plasterboard.

'That's a relief, because I don't want to be hounded out of town for a second time.'

A reluctant smile now curved Emily's lips. She actually began to feel a twinge of sympathy for James Bradshaw. So what if he had been playing the field six years ago in West Hampton? It was no more than a lot of young men did while they were growing up.

Now she was older, and she hoped a bit wiser, she could step back from the situation and see it from James's point of view. He had been far too young for commitment.

'The incident probably taught you a lesson.' Emily allowed a note of teasing to enter her voice.

'What sort of lesson?' James enquired with interest.

'Never underestimate anyone.'

'I hope I've never done that,' James spoke slowly, 'but with you around to remind me, I'm hardly like to forget, am I?'

Although Emily sensed she had won her first battle with James Bradshaw, it was important not to let victory go to her head. She had been reading up about his business methods in the financial press and she knew if her performance didn't come up to standard then he would follow up his threat to close down the theatre without a second thought.

'I'll do my best not to disappoint you, Mr Bradshaw,' she promised.

'Good,' he said and put out his hand, 'and it's James, Emily.'

The last time Emily had touched James, it had been to deliver a stinging blow to his face. From the expression in James's eyes, Emily had the suspicion that incident was another one he had not forgotten.

'We've Got A Reprieve'

'Over here, sweetie.' Lottie gestured to Toby as he strolled towards his studio. The sun cut a swathe of light across the lawn as the ducks circled the pond. 'Landy, fix the poor darling a drink, he looks totally exhausted.'

'Not for me, thanks,' Toby turned down the offer. 'I need to freshen up first.'

'Had a busy day, my sweet?' Lottie swirled ice cubes around in her glass.

'You could say that.' Toby eased himself into one of the wrought iron seats.

'They work you too hard at the club.' Lottie stroked his arm. 'Are you sure I can't tempt you with something?'

'Actually, I think I will change my mind if that's fresh orange on offer.'

Toby eyed the jug of liquid nestling in a bucket of ice.

'Good lad.' Orlando filled up a glass for him and passed it over.

'I don't suppose my agent called?' Toby asked hopefully.

'Sorry.' Orlando shook his head. 'Phone hasn't rung at all. That's why Lottie is so restless. She's been stuck with me all day.'

'Then there's been nothing from Emily either?'

'From what I hear the poor girl has been too busy to be in touch with anyone.'

'I was hoping someone might have fallen out of the next production and there's a spare director doing the rounds, desperately in need of my services as third spear-carrier from the left. Still, I expect she's got better things on her mind.'

'You're right, young Toby. Not sure there's going to be any more productions.' Orlando sounded unusually gloomy. 'James Bradshaw is an astute businessman. If he's decided the theatre's got to close then it will be curtains for us all.'

'Poor Emily,' Lottie sighed. 'I hope she's taken plenty of vitamins because she's certainly going to need them dealing with James Bradshaw. I'll never understand what possessed Joe to sell out to that wretched man.'

'James is a tough cookie,' Toby agreed, 'but you know for all her slenderness and charm Emily isn't exactly a shrinking violet. I've seen her lay into some lazy lumps of scene shifters. They were quaking in their overalls.'

Orlando guffawed. 'Good old Em. She's a great girl. The Alhambra will be in great hands if she wins the day.'

'Let's hope so. The meeting was today, wasn't it?' Toby asked.

'What meeting?' Lottie demanded, her violet eyes full of intrigue. 'Do tell.'

'To decide on The Little Alhambra's future.'

'You don't mean with James Bradshaw?' Lottie looked aghast. 'Why didn't she tell me? I should have been there to comfort her.'

Orlando raised his eyebrows at Toby. Much as they loved Lottie both men knew she was the last person Emily would have wanted around the place when she was composing her report.

A few moments of silence fell on the trio as they sipped their drinks on the terrace, each lost in their own thoughts while the evening closed in around them.

'We had Tricia Longfellow doing a radio programme in the club today,' Toby said changing the subject.

'Tricia Longfellow?' Lottie's eyes widened with surprise.

'Do you know her?' Toby asked.

'I know of her,' Lottie replied. 'She's Monty Smith's niece.'

'She mentioned something about an uncle, but she didn't say who he was. Mind you,' Toby added with a roguish grin, 'I didn't let on you were my aunt.'

'Very wise,' Orlando nodded agreement. 'Claiming kinship to Lottie is not always a wise move.'

'I don't know what you two are sniggering about,' Lottie complained. 'Anyone would think I had a reputation.'

'So you don't regard having had two husbands and a high profile relationship with a minor member of the aristocracy, not to mention being the most famous actress of a generation as a reputation?' Toby teased his aunt.

Lottie smiled happily. This was the sort of conversation she enjoyed.

'I've done nothing to be ashamed of,' she protested, 'compared to some of the things the other girls of my generation got up to I was positively angelic.' She raised her eyes in a theatrical gesture of innocence.

'Will you marry me all over again?' Orlando demanded.

'No,' Lottie replied.

'Why not? Fifteen years of marriage, but our wedding was so small. I'd love to do it again properly.'

'We've been through this dozens of

times, Landy, darling. We're quite happy and you know I'm rather unconventional and don't like the idea of a big wedding. Let's leave it at that.'

'Scaredy cat.' Toby grinned. 'You know Orlando's potty about you, why don't you just do it for him?'

'You haven't exactly rushed down the altar with any of your numerous lady friends,' Lottie retorted.

'Don't try and change the subject, Aunty Lottie.'

'Lottie will do. Much more of this backchat and I shall have to have words with your mother.'

'I only call you Aunty to annoy you,' Toby's eyes twinkled. 'By the way, what exactly has Monty Smith done to upset the locals? I keep hearing his name mentioned in hushed tones.'

'He developed Harley's Point, isn't that enough?' Orlando retorted.

'It's brought a lot of business to the area.'

'He'll be about the only person in West Hampton apart from James

Bradshaw who would welcome the closure of The Alhambra.'

'Right,' Toby nodded. 'I suppose he would. He's probably drawing up some hideous plans right now to convert the site into a ghastly amusement arcade.'

Orlando shuddered.

'When I think,' Lottie looked distressed, 'of the history attached to The Little Alhambra, it's criminal to think of pulling the building down. The Little Alhambra is a jewel in the crown.' She sat up straight. 'Landy, I've just had one of my brilliant ideas.'

'Oh no,' Orlando groaned.

'Why don't we set up some sort of action group to keep it open?'

'Now hold on,' Orlando said, 'I'd advise a bit of caution here, before we all get carried away.'

'I'm not getting carried away,' Lottie protested, 'but we can't sit around and do nothing. Dear Emily needs our support. She's a darling girl and she's done a lot to help put West Hampton on the map. It's our turn now to pay her back. We're not without influence, Landy. If we get some big names behind our campaign, James Bradshaw might be forced to think again. What do you think, boys?'

'I'm with Orlando on this one, Lottie,' Toby said. 'Caution is the name of the game. Besides you're supposed to have retired. You can't go gadding about the place at your age, getting involved in all sorts of hare-brained schemes.'

'Have I ever?' Lottie demanded.

'Yes,' Orlando and Toby replied in unison.

Lottie glared at the pair of them then conceded with a wry gesture of acknowledgement, 'I admit there were one or two occasions when things didn't go entirely according to plan but only due to circumstances beyond my control.'

'Exactly,' Orlando nodded. 'The last thing Emily needs is unasked for help. Besides, for all we know, James may agree to keep the theatre open. Let's wait until we hear an official decision before we do anything.'

'Neither of you are going to dampen my enthusiasm,' Lottie insisted. 'Besides I don't like sitting around all day doing nothing. Orlando,' she nudged him. There was a sly look in her eye as she said, 'you're putting on weight.'

'I am not,' Orlando protested. 'I've been the same weight for years.'

'Well,' Lottie pouted, 'you will get fat if you don't take any exercise.'

'I play golf and I mow the lawn.'

'On a tractor and you hire one of those buggy things on the golf course.'

'Stop bickering you two,' Toby remonstrated with the pair of them.

'Sorry,' Lottie apologised. 'I'm only feeling scratchy 'cos I'm worried about Emily.'

'I suppose it wouldn't do any harm to give her a call,' Toby admitted.

'The meeting must be over now,' Orlando agreed as he looked at his watch. 'You've got her mobile number haven't you, Toby?'

'Let me shower first.' Toby got to his feet.

'Invite her over to dinner,' Lottie insisted. 'I feel like some young company. Tell her Manuela's got fresh crab from the fish market today. Orlando, dig up a few new potatoes. Off you go. Work off some of that flab.'

* * *

'Em?' Toby was towelling down his damp hair as he answered the call. 'I was going to ring you in a few minutes. How did it go?'

'We've got a reprieve.' Her voice was an excited squeak.

'That's terrific,' Toby congratulated her. 'Well done, you. How on earth did you manage it? I thought you and James Bradshaw were sworn enemies.'

'It was a bit touch and go at times,' she admitted. 'At one point, I even offered my resignation.'

'You didn't?' Toby repeated in amazement.

'Luckily James didn't accept it. He's given me until the beginning of next year to turn things round. If I fail, then that's it.'

'That's pretty fair,' Toby agreed, 'and you won't fail. Everyone's right behind you on this one. Listen, you have to celebrate.'

'I haven't got time,' Emily insisted.

'Yes you have,' Toby was equally firm. 'Lottie said to tell you there's fresh crab and some of Orlando's new potatoes on the menu here at Pippins tonight. I bet you haven't eaten a thing all day have you?'

'I had an apple for lunch,' Emily replied, 'I think.'

After their meeting James had insisted on a guided tour of the theatre, during which he had fired so many questions at Emily, her head still ached from the pressure.

'Then you need something more substantial for dinner. Besides which,' Toby lowered his voice, 'you have got to come. There's this girl who's making

87

herself a bit of a nuisance. I'm trying to cool things between us but she might call in tonight. If she sees you and me together, she may back off a bit.'

'Toby,' Emily remonstrated with him, 'you are heartless and it's time you settled down with a proper girl.'

'Will you marry me?'

'No I will not.'

'Thought you'd say that,' Toby grinned. 'Orlando and I don't have much luck on the proposal front.'

Emily smiled. She had known Toby on and off for years, from the days when he used to spend his summer holidays with Lottie. Over time their relationship had developed into one of deep friendship.

'And another thing, I'm going to have to give up playing your girlfriend, Toby,' Emily insisted, 'I'll be too busy.'

'Be that as it may, I really think you ought to have dinner with us tonight, Em, because Lottie's talking about setting up an action support group.'

'What?'

'Exactly.'

'Couldn't you talk her out of it?'

'Orlando and I tried, but she wasn't in the mood to listen and you know what she's like when she gets a bee in her bonnet. I thought maybe you could use your charm on her? Please? Come on, it's been ages since you paid us a visit.'

'Well I was going to open a can of soup, but crab and new potatoes does sound very tempting.'

'Great. Want me to come and get you? I could borrow Orlando's Bentley.'

'Last time you tried that, it got stuck on the hill, remember?'

'Vividly,' Toby shuddered.

'It took three strong men to shift it.'

'Why you have to live in a converted fisherman's cottage in the old part of the town I will never know.'

'I like it here, besides it's got charm, unlike that soulless Harley's Point of Monty Smith's. I'll get a taxi. See you at eight?'

'Eight it is.'

Blowing a kiss down the phone, Toby switched off. Emily would need all the help she could get in the coming months and he hoped to be there for her.

A Reunion On The Beach
With James

Emily could hear the sound of children playing on the beach through her open window. It was something that always gladdened her heart. With the impending approach of summer, business at West Hampton was picking up.

Benito had long since handed over the reins of his entertainment empire to a younger generation, and already a squad of nephews and grandsons was busy erecting kiosks and sorting out the café and ice cream parlour in time for the new season. Soon the seafront would be throbbing with life, all of which gave Emily a feel good buzz.

She turned her reluctant attention back to her laptop. It was difficult to concentrate on work when the sun was streaming through the window. The sky was brilliant blue and she longed to go for a walk barefoot along the beach and feel wet sand ooze between her toes and listen to the waves lapping the shore, but it was Saturday morning and one of the busiest days of the year.

The first new production since James had taken over the theatre was due to start the following week. Much to Toby's delight Emily had been asked by the director to offer him the starring role as, due to a clash of commitments, the previous leading man had been forced to drop out.

'No kidding,' Toby had responded with a loud whoop when she had telephoned him. Emily had been obliged to move the receiver away from her ear as his shout of delight threatened to shatter her eardrums. 'I owe you one. This could be my big break. I've never played the lead before.'

'It's only for a week,' Emily pointed out.

'A week is a long time in our business,' Toby replied.

Learning his lines had taken up most of Toby's spare time during the past week and Emily was relieved not to be dragooned into her usual role-play of acting up as his girlfriend. Word was being put around the crowd she mixed with that she and Toby were an item, a situation she was anxious to defuse.

Emily liked Toby. He was good company, but their relationship was no more than that of good friends. Toby could be flaky and wasn't the sort to stay faithful to one woman for any length of time. Emily had personal experience as to what that sort of relationship could do to her, which was why, at the age of twenty five she was still foot loose and fancy free.

There had been other boyfriends since James Bradshaw but Emily was careful not to let them develop into anything serious.

It had been ten days since her meeting with James, during which time her feet had hardly touched the ground. The last week of May was carnival week and signified the official start of the summer season at West Hampton. Emily intended to use the occasion to publicise the theatre's summer programme and she had persuaded the local school to help with the decoration of a float.

Emily inspected the online status of seat availability. The forward bookings looked good and next week's 'cosy' crime caper would play to packed houses. Toby was a great local attraction and she knew the presence of his name on the cast list would be an added bonus. Coupled with that of the minor soap star who was playing the role of the romantic interest, Emily sensed they were on to a winner.

The carnival week always attracted significant media attention and Emily intended to ensure The Alhambra featured prominently in all the advance publicity.

During their quiet time Ted had set

about refurbishing the theatre. He had dug out the Chinese lanterns again. Ivy had given them a face-lift and they were now a permanent feature of the ornamental gardens. The façade of the old theatre had been given a lick of paint and all the fairy lights overhauled. Ivy had weeded the flowerbeds and the hanging baskets had received a new lease of life.

A loud rapping on the door of her cottage made Emily jump. She looked up at the clock and saw it was nearly midday. She hoped it wasn't Toby come to ask her out to lunch. His lunches always extended well into the afternoon and at the moment Emily didn't have that sort of time to spare.

She peered out of her upstairs window to spy on whoever was standing on the steps. If it was Toby she fully intended not to answer the door.

A tall figure was standing in the middle of the cobble-stoned street looking up at her window. There was no time to duck down, or pretend she was out.

'Hi there.' James looked up at her.

He was wearing a white T shirt and paint-stained jeans and looked remarkably bronzed and carefree. Emily's heart contracted at the sight of him. He hardly looked a day older than when he had been working for Benito during the long hot summer of their affair.

Yet six years had passed, six years during which Emily had done her best not to think about the man that had broken her heart. She must remember that this same man was now a hard-headed businessman with no thought but where the next penny was coming from.

'Er, hello,' she returned his greeting.

'Are you coming down?' James asked, 'or would you like me to stand here and shout up at you like a lovesick swain?' His almond shaped eyes were full of mischief. 'I don't mind,' he added, 'but it would mean everyone else in Fisherman's Lane would hear what I have to say and some of it is of a personal nature.'

Emily flushed with embarrassment. She could already see Miss Simpson opposite twitching her lace curtains. She was the nosiest neighbour in the world and loved nothing better than poking her nose into other people's affairs.

'What do you want?' Emily hissed anxious not to be overheard.

'It's such a lovely day I was going to suggest a walk along the beach.'

The chink in Miss Simpson's curtains grew wider and Emily could see her face, as she made no secret of peering through the gap.

'I haven't got time for a walk,' Emily protested.

'I won't go away until you agree to come downstairs and talk to me properly,' James insisted.

Emily could see he meant business.

'Sorry.' She was breathless by the time she opened her front door.

James's blue eyes widened as he took in the flowery sundress and the daisy sandals.

'So the walk's on, is it?' James said to Emily.

'I shouldn't really,' Emily protested again. 'I've a mountain of work to get through.'

'This is work too. Think of it as an open-air update meeting. Ready?'

Something in the tone of James's voice told her he wasn't going to take no for an answer.

'All right. I could do with a break.'

Emily closed her front door and together she and James strolled down the winding hill towards the harbour. They turned in the direction of the bandstand.

'You're looking pale,' James said as Emily averted her eyes from the scene of their last vitriolic encounter. 'When did you last have a day off?'

'I can't remember, but I don't mind. I love what I do,' Emily insisted.

'All the same I don't want your health to suffer.'

'Worried about your investment?' Emily knew his concern was no more than professional, 'well there's no need to be.'

James stopped walking and looked so hard at her she began to feel uncomfortable.

'What's the matter?' she was goaded into demanding as the silence between them stretched into minutes.

'Perhaps I was wrong,' he admitted slowly.

'About what?' Emily asked, a feeling of apprehension creeping up her backbone.

'The nine months' reprieve.'

'You can't back out now. I've signed my copy of the contract.' Two days after their meeting, Emily had received an official document from James's solicitors, outlining the details of their agreement.

'I've no intention of backing out.' James insisted, 'but perhaps I should leave things as they are and let The Alhambra struggle on without imposing any provisos.'

'No.'

Emily's raised voice startled the

circling seagulls.

'That's a pretty fierce denial,' James laughed. 'What brought it on?'

'I don't want any favours,' Emily insisted.

'All right then,' James agreed, 'as you feel so strongly about it, we'll keep the status quo as it is.'

'Thank you. It's very difficult to keep anything quiet in a small community like West Hampton and people would start to talk if they learned you'd gone back on your deal.'

'What you're also saying is they would also start wondering if there was anything between us?'

Emily began to feel uncomfortably warm. They were straying too far into personal territory.

'It's possible,' she mumbled.

'And we wouldn't want that would we?'

Emily turned her face away from the teasing expression in his eyes. 'I don't believe in mixing business with plea-sure,' she replied, aware she sounded rather like a prim schoolteacher lecturing a recalcitrant pupil.

'The tide's out, fancy a walk along the sand?' James suggested after a short pause.

Emily's heart thumped as she remembered past walks on the sand. For a moment she considered turning down his offer, pleading pressure of work, but the expression in James's eyes got the better of her.

'All right.'

She removed her daisy-decorated sandals and dangling them from her fingers, walked barefoot down the steps leading to the beach. James followed her and as they stood on the sand staring at each other, the years rolled away.

'Race you to the breakwater?' Emily challenged him and laughing set off before he had time to remove his trainers.

'Hey, come back. That's not fair,' he panted after her, 'you started before me.'

'You've got longer legs,' she called over her shoulder.

Not looking where she was going, the next moment she tripped and fell flat on her face in the sand. Sprawled amongst the remains of a child's sandcastle, she could hear James laughing as he pounded past her.

'Bad luck. I win,' he crowed as he perched on the breakwater and waited for her to catch him. 'You look a mess,' he added as she struggled upright and attempted to brush damp sand off her arms and legs.

'You cheated.'

'I didn't,' he protested. 'You were the unsporting one who roared off like a rocket leaving me in the starting stalls.'

Emily grinned back at him. 'Well, in this world you've got to fight dirty sometimes.'

'Yes,' he agreed slowly, 'I suppose you have to.'

James was again looking at her with such intensity she was forced to transfer her gaze out to the horizon. She wondered if she had been the first in a long string of hearts he had broken and how often he had fought dirty.

'Do you know what happened to Lucy Jackson?' he asked.

'Last I heard she was married with three children,' Emily replied.

'You've never thought of getting married?' James asked.

Emily shook her head. 'I haven't been engaged either.'

'Me neither. So, how have you spent the last six years?'

'I went to college, then after my parents sold up their bed and breakfast business and moved to Minorca I started temporary work at The Alhambra until Joe took me on as manager.'

'You didn't want to broaden your horizons away from West Hampton?'

'No.'

'It does have a strange pull doesn't it?'

Emily turned back to face him. 'Is that why you came back?' she asked.

'Is what why I came back?' James

moved closer towards her.

'Was the pull of West Hampton too great to resist? Or was it the memory of Benito's ice cream and the Sunday afternoon concerts?'

Her attempt at a joke turned a little flat as James said in a soft voice, 'Something drew me back and I don't think it was the double choc chip.'

Above them the seagulls keened. In the distance Emily could see a speed-boat darting over the waves trailing a water skier in its wake. The sand was gritty between her toes. It was so like the old days Emily could feel her resistance to James wavering. He was close enough now for her to smell his aftershave.

'There you are.' A voice behind them made Emily jump. 'I've been looking for you everywhere. We had a date. Don't tell me you'd forgotten.'

A stunning girl wearing a white top and yellow shorts that displayed long tanned limbs strolled towards them.

'Good heavens,' her eyes widened at

the state of Emily's stained sundress. 'What on earth have you been doing, wrestling with a sand castle?'

'I fell over,' Emily replied.

'Aren't you Emily Sinclair?'

'Yes. I am.'

'Tricia Longfellow.'

Emily shook Tricia's hand. 'If you'll excuse me I think I'd better go home and change.'

'Good idea.' She turned her back on Emily. 'Now, James, where are you going to take me for that lunch you promised me?'

Not even bothering to say goodbye, Emily walked as slowly as her dignity would allow, back towards the beach steps. For a moment she had almost been taken in by James's charm, but nothing had changed. He was still the same two-timing player he has always been. She was grateful Tricia Longfellow had come along when she had and broken things up between them.

As she trailed up the steps Emily remembered now where she'd heard the name Tricia Longfellow before. She was Monty Smith's niece. It was inevitable she and James would know each other. They were in the same business and judging from the closeness of Tricia's body language they were more than just business acquaintances.

She tossed her hair out of her eyes. At least Tricia had saved her from making a fool of herself. She had been dangerously close to trusting James Bradshaw for the second time in her life and that was a mistake she had absolutely no intention of repeating.

Emily Accuses James Of Making Trouble

'We've got problems, Emily.' Ted was patrolling the theatre forecourt on Monday morning waiting for her. His greeting struck a chord of dismay in Emily's chest.

She had spent the best part of Sunday wondering if James and Tricia Longfellow were in league with each other and she didn't need further reasons to arouse her suspicions.

'What sort of problems?' she asked carefully taking in his worried expression.

'Were you in yesterday?'

'I worked from home. Why?'

Emily ignored the feeling of guilt niggling her conscience. James had telephoned her early on in the morning and mentioned he might check up on the theatre during the afternoon to see how things were going. In a fit of pique Emily decided to stay out of his way.

If James wanted to snoop there was nothing she could do to stop him. No mention had been made of his lunch date with Tricia or of their walk along the beach and Emily ignored the small voice in her head, suggesting she was acting a bit like a spoilt child. James was perfectly entitled to have relation-ships with whomsoever he wished.

'Well someone was in,' Ted was speaking again. 'Come and see.'

Emily followed him through to The Green Room, the backstage hub of the theatre where the actors could relax between scenes. The Green Room was always kept freshly decorated. The surfaces were clutter free and gleamed from Ivy's regular polishing and dust-ing, but not today.

'Who could have done this?' Emily demanded.

'Search me.' Ted scratched the back

of his head as they looked at the mess.

Someone had raided the wardrobe and emptied every costume out and strewn them artistically over the chairs. They weren't damaged in any way but the carpet was littered with cocktail dresses, ball gowns, doublets, hose, even a pitchfork.

'Thank heavens we don't keep all our stock here,' Emily murmured as she retrieved one of the dresses and replaced it on a hanger.

'And thank goodness there's no other damage,' Ted added. 'In fact it's been a very tidy break in.'

It was an unwritten rule that The Green Room should be kept in a pristine condition as a mark of respect to the founder of the theatre.

'Leaves a nasty feeling in the mouth, something like this, doesn't it?'

Emily nodded.

'We'll have to think about some night security,' Ted looked gloomy again. 'I mean we don't want a repeat performance of this sort of thing especially if a production's in progress.'

'This is West Hampton,' Emily protested. 'Heavy security has never been necessary before.'

'We've never played to such high stakes before,' Ted pointed out.

'I suppose you're right.' Emily agreed with him.

'Do we have to inform the police?' Ted asked in a reluctant voice.

'Since no real damage was done I suppose it isn't strictly necessary, but Mr Bradshaw will need to know.' It was against Emily's better judgement but it was only fair to James to keep him informed of this latest development to befall the theatre.

'If Mr Bradshaw takes against it, it could go badly for us,' Ted voiced Emily's worst fears.

James had admitted that propping up a failing, accident bound, old theatre was not his style and this sort of incident would be exactly the excuse he was looking for to carry out his threat of closure. He would leap on it as an example of why they were no longer viable and he wouldn't fail to use it to his advantage.

'If you like,' Ted suggested, 'I could camp here tonight in case whoever it was does decide to come back and have another go.'

'Ted,' Emily protested, 'I can't ask you to do that.'

'The old place is quite cosy in the dark and it wouldn't be the first time I've done it. I'll rig up my camp bed and I've got a little heater to keep me warm and there's always the ghost light to protect me,' he joked, 'so I won't be completely in the dark. Don't worry,' he intercepted her frown of concern, 'you can trust me not to set fire to the place either.'

'I'm not worried about that, Ted,' she assured him uncertain how to voice her misgivings without hurting his feelings.

Ted was of stocky build and capable of taking care of himself, but there was no way he could hold his own against a younger man, intent on making mischief.

'Darling, the door was open so I hope you don't mind me dropping in.'

There was a waft of familiar French perfume and the sound of swishing silk as Lottie appeared in the doorway. Emily stifled a feeling of irritation. Lottie was not exactly the most discreet person in the world and if she got a whiff of what had happened here, it would be all over the seafront in seconds.

The violet eyes widened in surprise as she took in the scene of devastation.

'Has Hamlet has been up to his old tricks again?' she asked.

'Hamlet?' Emily frowned at her.

Lottie gave a girlish giggle. 'My nickname for the ghost,' she explained to an equally puzzled Ted.

'Haven't time for any of that nonsense,' he muttered.

'Every theatre's got one, a ghost. It's traditional,' Lottie insisted.

Emily knew theatre folk were notoriously superstitious and the list of things you weren't supposed to do was legion — no fresh flowers, or mirrors, no whistling or knitting and the use of peacock feathers was not to be permitted. The carrying of a make-up box for some reason was also deemed unlucky. Lottie came from a background that believed in theatre folklore. Emily did not.

'I remember once when I was playing the . . . '

'Lottie,' Emily cut short her reminiscences.

'Yes, darling?'

'We don't want word of what has happened here getting out.'

'I understand completely, sweetie and you know me, I am the soul of discretion.'

Discretion and Lottie did not live in the same sentence but Emily had too much on her mind to make an issue of it.

'If there's anything I can do to help?' Lottie offered. 'The reason I popped in to see you was to talk about the

Carnival. It's next week, isn't it?'

'That's all in hand, Lottie,' Emily assured her.

'Excellent. I thought perhaps a little party chez moi afterwards might be in order? You know how Landy adores a bash and it would generate lots more lovely publicity. We could open up the gardens and invite the media? You could bring James along with you and introduce him to some of our regulars.'

'The party is a wonderful idea, Lottie, but if you decide to invite James he can come by himself,' Emily insisted.

'It would make sense for the two of you to come together, wouldn't it?'

'We are not an item.'

'I thought you were beginning to rekindle your relationship.'

'Whatever gave you that idea?'

'Molly Simpson says he called on you last Saturday morning and was quite insistent that you join him for a walk along the beach. You changed into a pretty sundress and you were seen by one of the seafront chefs too so it's no use denying it,' Lottie added with a smile.

'It was a business meeting,' Emily insisted wondering how anyone managed to keep anything quiet in West Hampton.

'If you say so.' Lottie didn't look in the least bit convinced. 'But you know, I don't think James Bradshaw is as bad as he's painted.'

'Did I hear someone mention my name?' a voice interrupted Lottie before Emily could reply.

With a sinking heart she looked over Lottie's shoulder to see James standing behind her in the doorway to The Green Room.

'Good heavens, James,' Lottie gave a nervous start, 'don't creep up on me like that. It's not good for my heart.'

'No-one was in the office. I tried ringing the bell in the foyer but that didn't work either. Where is everybody?'

Lottie's mobile trilled into life and created a welcome distraction.

'Hello? Yes? Er, it's not frightfully

convenient at the moment.' Lottie lowered her voice. 'I'm actually at the theatre now.' She turned a deeper shade of pink and cast a guilty glance in Emily's direction. Moving away from her and James she continued her conversation in a hushed voice.

James advanced into the room. His cool blue eyes took in the scene of devastation around them then.

'What on earth has been going on?' he demanded.

'Nothing.' Emily tried to make light of the matter.

'It doesn't look like nothing to me. Has there been a break-in?'

'Yes. No. I'm not sure.'

Right now all Emily wanted was a few moments on her own to get her head together, but she could tell from the set of James's jawline that he was in no mood to leave.

'Got to go.' Lottie finished her call and dropped her mobile back into her bag. 'Now don't forget if you need any help, you know where to find me and

116

make sure you keep your costumes under lock and key in future. We don't want the theatre burning down do we?'

'Has there been a fire?' James demanded.

Lottie fluttered her eyelashes. It was always a sign she was nervous and Emily began to suspect she knew more about what had happened here than she was prepared to let on.

'No, nothing like that. It's just that there's a rumour that the ghost sometimes leaves the flat iron on.'

'What ghost?' James demanded.

'I really must go.' Lottie began edging out of the door.

She blew them a kiss before disappearing into the auditorium. The door to the foyer slammed shut behind her.

'What was all that about?' James asked with a puzzled frown.

'Some nonsense Lottie dreamed up about a ghost. There are all sorts of stories about supernatural sightings in every theatre. I pay no attention to them,' Emily replied trying to make light of things.

'Neither would I. Someone human broke in and did this.'

'No, they didn't.'

'Surely you don't believe it was a ghost?' James swept a hand in the direction of the discarded costumes.

'Whoever it was they must have had a key. Ted says there's been no sign of a forced entry.'

'You think a key holder is responsible?'

'What other explanation is there?'

James moved towards her and for one moment Emily thought he was going to touch her face.

'I have a key,' he said softly.

'And you were here on your own yesterday afternoon, weren't you?' Emily did her best to keep her voice steady.

'This is nothing to do with me, Emily. Surely you don't think that? I can assure you I locked up after I left and I still have my key on me.'

James dangled his fob in front of her.

'It doesn't take a degree in rocket science to work out where the costumes are kept and to fling a few of them about the place.'

'Why would I do that?'

'Isn't it obvious?'

'Not to me it isn't.'

'Tricia Longfellow.'

James shook his head in puzzlement. 'You're going to have to give me more than that.'

'Did she offer you a deal on her uncle's behalf if the theatre closed down?'

'No.'

'How do I know that?'

'Do I need to prove to you that I'm telling the truth?'

'The last time I saw the pair of you together you were cosying up like old friends.'

'And you think we were hatching a plot to discredit The Alhambra?'

'Were you?' Emily knew she was behaving irrationally but where James Bradshaw was concerned her behaviour had never been rational. 'Her uncle is Monty Smith. He may have asked his niece to sound you out.'

'Perhaps Monty Smith has strayed a bit close to the wind occasionally but I don't think he's ever been guilty of intimidation and if I were you, Emily, I should be very careful not to repeat that allegation in public.'

Emily began to feel uncomfortably warm. 'Perhaps that was a little hasty of me,' she backtracked.

'For your further information I have never cosied up to Tricia Longfellow. Last Saturday was the first time I had met her.'

'She said you had a lunch date.'

'That was news to me but I really don't have the time to stand here arguing with you about Monty Smith and his niece. What I do need is your promise that you won't start playing detective and prowling around the theatre on your own after dark.'

'Why not? I can look after myself.'

'I very much doubt you could hold

your own if there is someone bent on mischief. Whoever he is, he may not be too particular about lashing out if he's cornered.'

The expression in James's eyes was now so intense Emily could only mumble in reply, 'There's no need for you to worry. Ted has offered to camp out overnight to keep an eye on things.'

'Right, good idea. I'll have a word with him before I leave and make sure he's got my mobile number. By the way, how many people have keys to the theatre?'

'Only three of us, you, me and Ted.'

'Then I suggest you get the locks changed because somehow someone seems to have got their hands on a fourth key.'

Emily nodded. At least James hadn't gone so far as to accuse her or Ted. She bit her lip in consternation realising she had not been so considerate towards James.

In the distance she could hear her telephone ringing in the office. Emily forced herself not to flinch as James's fingers grazed her cheek. 'You've got a bit of cotton from one of the costumes in your hair,' he tweaked it free and disposed of it in a wastepaper bin then turned back to her. 'I never realised life in the theatre was quite this exciting.'

Emily's smile was a little shaky as she responded with, 'Wait until dress rehearsal night.'

'Promise me that you won't do anything silly?' James asked softly. 'We don't know what we're dealing with here. Leave it to Ted and me, please?'

Emily nodded reluctantly. 'But if there's any action I want to be in on it,' she added.

'I wouldn't have expected anything else,' James replied with a wry twist to his mouth. 'If there's no recurrence tonight, I'll be in again tomorrow to check up on things.'

Back in her office Emily snatched up the receiver.

'Hi,' a cheerful voice greeted her down the line, 'Tricia Longfellow here.'

Emily Denies A Romance
With Toby

James and Emily were squashed together far too close for comfort in the confined space of the radio display stand. All around them carnival chaos reigned. Brass band music blared out from a loud-speaker as float after float trundled along the seafront to waves of applause and loud cheers.

The promenade hummed with activity. Benito's was doing a roaring trade in ice creams and soft drinks and the seagulls were having a field day as they swooped down on the remains of discarded cornets and picnics.

'Is it always this manic?' James demanded as a drum roll heralded another round of deafening cheers.

'You wait and see,' Emily warned

him, 'things haven't really got going yet.'

James raised his eyebrows. 'Now you tell me,' he said with the faintest trace of a smile. 'There have to be more comfortable ways of spending a baking Saturday afternoon than being cooped up in a squawk box.'

'You volunteered for this job.'

'I seem to remember it was you who volunteered me. What on earth is that digging in my back?' James wriggled about as he tried to get comfortable. 'Are you sure this contraption isn't some form of medieval torture instrument?'

'It was actually Tricia Longfellow's idea.'

'Remind me never to speak to her again.'

'She said you told her that the carnival might be a good opportunity to raise your local community profile.'

'I don't remember saying anything of the sort,' James protested.

'Then that's something you'll have to

take up with Tricia, won't you?' Emily couldn't resist teasing him. 'I knew the pair of you were up to something.'

'For the last time, we were not up to anything,' James insisted.

The carnival was essentially a family occasion and the atmosphere of the day was getting to Emily. She grinned at James. The parade was always fun and the sight of his tall frame crouched in the stuffy confines of a broadcasting box doing battle with the fixtures and fittings was the icing on the cake.

'You do look funny,' she teased as yet another piece of equipment attacked him.

'I do not look funny and I'm glad you're finding my appearance a source of amusement,' James retaliated. 'You'll understand if I don't join in the general hilarity.'

'Don't be so grumpy,' she chided him and leaning forward she picked some wood shavings off his shirt. 'There is that better?'

Realising being too close to James

was an error of judgement, Emily backed off immediately.

'Scared the equipment is going to get you too?' The reaction was not lost on James.

'I thought you looked as though you needed body space.'

It was a feeble explanation but the best Emily could do given the circumstances.

'You're right, I do. How do you manage to look so cool in this steam bath?'

'I've done it before,' she informed him.

'Well I wish you'd told me. I'd have worn my bathing shorts.'

Emily tried to concentrate on the job in hand. She was beginning to regret having been talked into this job but Tricia Longfellow was nothing if not persuasive.

'I was about to ring off,' she had informed Emily over the telephone.

'If you want to speak to James I'm afraid you've just missed him.' It had been difficult for Emily to keep the coolness out of her voice.

'It's you I want to talk to,' Tricia replied, 'about the carnival. I tried to get James interested when we had lunch together, well actually it was only a snatched sandwich on the seafront. He's a difficult person to get hold of, isn't he?'

'I'm sorry?' Emily sank into her chair. She realised she was still clutching one of the theatre's costumes and now the fuss following the break in had died down she also realised her legs were shaking badly and in need of support.

'I've been trying to track him down for ages. I virtually lived in the lift at Harley's Point after Toby told me James occupied the penthouse. I tell you I was beginning to attract some very strange looks from the porter. I was about to give up hope when I spotted him down by the beach last Saturday morning.'

Tricia paused for breath.

Emily remained silent hoping she

would get to the point.

'Anyway, when I saw you were covered in sand and seaweed I knew you'd welcome the chance to freshen up so I invented a date with him to let you off the hook.' Tricia's light laugh trilled down the line. 'James was too much of a gentleman to turn me down when I suggested lunch.'

'Right,' Emily said, wondering where this was going and ignoring the wave of relief caused by Tricia's explanation.

Why she should care if Tricia and James were an item, she didn't know, but annoying though it was, she did.

'Sorry, you're probably immensely busy and I'm wasting your time.'

'Not at all,' Emily insisted drawing on her professionalism. 'The Alhambra is always pleased to speak to local radio.'

'The thing is, my date with James was a bit of a non event. It wasn't even a date really. James seemed distracted. He kept looking over my shoulder as if he was expecting you to reappear or something and the whole time I had to keep repeating myself.

'That sort of thing does nothing for a girl's ego I can tell you. Anyway, what I want to know is would the pair of you be interested in manning the mobile radio station together for say, a couple of hours, during the carnival parade? I know you've done stints in the past and it would be excellent publicity for the theatre.'

'What would you want us to do?'

'Play a bit of music, commentate and interview anyone who looks interesting, that sort of thing.'

'I'd be pleased to,' Emily began.

'Great,' Tricia enthused.

'I'm not sure about James though. He's a bit publicity-shy.'

'Use your charm on him. I'm sure he'll listen to you. I got absolutely nowhere so I'm relying on you.'

'I'll see what I can do but I'm not making any promises.'

Emily realised it would be foolish to let their personal agenda jeopardise the success of the carnival which explained why she and James were now the presenters of the Carnival Radio Special Parade Programme. Emily wriggled as she tried to get comfortable on the miniscule stool the organisers had provided. There was another dull thud and a muffled curse as James banged his head.

'Careful,' Emily hissed.

'It's all very well for you,' James glared at her, 'I'm twice as tall as you.'

'You're also on air.'

'What?' James put a quick hand over the loudspeaker to cover his gaffe.

'Hope you don't get arrested by the carnival constables for bad language.'

'You're enjoying this, aren't you?' James accused Emily.

'Lighten up. Remember we are doing our bit for the community,' she reminded him, 'and aren't you supposed to be commentating on the parade?'

'Not while the music's playing.'

'Watch out. It's coming to an end. We're on.'

'Ladies first.' James wriggled out of

her way as Emily took up the microphone.

'Coward,' she said as she swung into the routine she had practised in front of her bedroom mirror after her bath last night.

'Ladies and gentlemen, I'm Emily Sinclair and it's my pleasure to welcome you to this year's West Hampton Carnival. Aren't those floats something else?'

Her announcement was met with a loud round of applause. As one of the main sponsors, the local radio station had a prime site on the seafront and the crowds milling around outside were in places three and four deep. The carnival always attracted a huge attendance but this year's event was busier than ever due to the warm weather and the increased media coverage.

'Did you see the float for The Little Alhambra?' Another cheer went up. 'If you did and you can name all the fictional characters represented on the float, then you are in with a chance for a super prize. The theatre is offering one night's exclusive use of Lottie Moulin's private box. Not a prize to be sniffed at,' Emily paused, 'so get your thinking caps on, folks and enter the competition now.

'The float is about half way down the procession. To start you off, one of the characters is from this season's panto-mime. I'm giving nothing away but she's wearing a glass slipper. So there you have it. The prize draw will take place after tonight's performance when his Worship, the Mayor, has kindly agreed to officiate over the ceremony. Don't delay. Get your entry in now. We all want to keep The Alhambra open don't we?'

The response was deafening. 'Great stuff,' Emily responded, 'and to help things along this afternoon, I have West Hampton's very own superstar, James Bradshaw, with me. Over to you, James.'

'Superstar?' James mouthed at her in horror.

'Just wing it.' Emily put a swift hand over the microphone to stifle his groan as he tried to shift position. 'For goodness sake, what are you doing now?'

'This thing was built for a vertically challenged garden gnome.' There was a loud crack as James inadvertently kicked in one of the panels.

'That should make a great picture on the front of The Herald next week.' Emily giggled as his booted foot protruded through the hole he had made in the panelling.

Emily hadn't expected to enjoy her afternoon this much. She had half expected James to turn her down flat when she relayed Tricia's suggestion to him. When, to Emily's surprise, he had agreed, she began to have her doubts about his decision, but the only downside so far was being much too close to James in confined surroundings.

Press bulbs exploded as James took over the broadcast.

'Thank you ladies and gentlemen and thank you, Emily, for inviting me here today.' The smile he cast in her direction was so charming, it brought a flush to the base of her neck.

She knew it was for the benefit of the cameras, but even so it made her fingertips tingle. 'I know the carnival is going to be a big success and we want to make this year's event the best ever, don't we? Emily and I will be manning the radio stand all afternoon so come along and say hello to us. We'd love to see you.'

A troop of drum majorettes rounded the corner, drowning out what remained of James's speech. With a grimace of defeat he sat down again and watched them march past.

'What do I do now?'

'Put on some more music.'

He fumbled around for the right switch.

'I thought you'd done this sort of thing before,' Emily said, 'as part of your media training.'

'I have but not in a Punch and Judy box.'

Before Emily could reply she heard someone calling out her name. She squinted into the sunshine then waved enthusiastically at a passing float.

'Isn't that Toby French?' James asked as the Watersports Centre float rolled by followed by a trail of teenage girls carrying surfboards and wearing snorkelling equipment. 'What's he doing up there?'

'He works at the centre in his spare time.'

'I had no idea your boyfriend was so talented.'

'Toby is not my boyfriend.'

This was a conversation Emily had had many times with many people and she was anxious to dispel the rumours that she and Toby were an item.

'You're often seen together.'

'Why shouldn't we be? He's playing the lead in our new production.'

'That's not what I mean.'

'Not that it's any of your business,

135

but Toby and I go way back. He's like a brother. His mother is Lottie's sister and they always spent their holidays down here. Does that answer your questions?'

'You know,' James drew his lips together tightly, 'I wouldn't be surprised if Lottie Moulin wasn't behind that bit of disruption at the theatre.'

Luckily there had been no more incidents and Ted had reported nothing suspicious during the two nights he had camped out at The Alhambra.

'Don't let's get started on all that again,' Emily implored. 'Anyway, why on earth would Lottie vandalise the costumes?'

'There's no such thing as bad publicity and this ghost business has certainly drummed up local interest. It was on the front page of The Herald.'

'Then if Lottie was involved maybe she got it right. A front page spread is certainly cheaper than having to pay for an advert.'

'It's not ethical.'

Emily could feel her good humour evaporating. It was stuffy and growing steadily hotter in the radio stand and if James Bradshaw was going to sit beside her and make derogatory remarks about Lottie Moulin then she wanted out.

'Hi, guys, how's it going?' Toby poked his head round the door. 'My you look hot, James.'

'Toby,' Emily beamed at him then for James's benefit she kissed Toby on the cheek.

Toby raised his eyebrows in surprise. 'What was that for?' he asked. 'Am I in your good books?'

Ignoring James she continued smiling at Toby. 'Finished on the float have you?'

'The guys are getting a drink I might join them in a minute. I just came over to see if there's anything I can do to help.'

'It's Toby French, isn't it?' A young mother pushing a baby buggy approached him. 'Can we have your autograph?'

Toby signed her book with a flourish and subjected her to his best actor's smile. 'There you are.'

'Last week was the first time my husband's ever taken me to a play,' she said.

'Did you enjoy it?' Toby asked.

'I thought you were wonderful,' she gushed. 'I'm taking my mother to see the next production as a birthday treat.'

'That's what I like to hear. Tell all your friends about us, won't you. We've got to keep the theatre open, haven't we?'

'Nice one, Toby,' Emily congratulated him. 'Actually, there is something you can do.' She thrust a microphone under his nose. 'You can be our roving reporter. See if you can find anyone interesting to interview on the esplanade.'

'Knew it was a mistake to volunteer,' he grumbled, ducking his head as he departed. The crowds thronging around the stand immediately swallowed him up.

'That's the last you'll see of him this afternoon,' James predicted.

'Look, if you can't find anything good to say about Lottie or Toby I suggest you take the other microphone out and drum up some local publicity.'

'You mean I can leave?' James's face lit up.

'There's no need to look quite so enthusiastic about it.'

Emily flattened herself against one of the backboards as James scrambled past her.

'Sure you can manage?' He looked back at her.

Emily felt a twinge of guilt. James did look very hot and there was a film of sweat on his forehead.

'You get some fresh air.' The soft hair on his arm was springy to the touch as Emily inadvertently stroked it, 'and for goodness sake smile.'

'Yes ma'am. Will this do?' James responded with a smile that sent her blood pressure rocketing.

'Hi, I'm Carly Palermo.' A bubbly

blonde accosted him relieving Emily of the challenge of replying.

'Er, hello, Carly,' James smiled uncertainly.

'Leading lady for the summer show?' she prompted as he continued to look confused.

'Right, of course.' Recognition kicked in. 'Nice to meet you.'

Carly was the daughter of impresario Roger Palermo and Emily had no doubt that by the end of the summer, Carly's blonde beauty and breathy voice would have broken more than a few male hearts.

Toby And James Clash Over Emily

The carnival parade had gone well. Emily continued to man the radio stand all Saturday afternoon while James interviewed bystanders and mentioned the theatre at every opportunity. He proved surprisingly adept at coaxing the shyest of people into turning into a star act and there had been a lot of laughter during the programme. Tricia manning the control centre had been pleased with the feedback.

Toby had been obliged to leave early because of theatre commitments and in the evening he had done his stuff in front of the mayor, earning warm applause for his performance as the slightly naughty but lovable romantic lead in the frothy farce chosen to complement the carnival.

The post performance party had been held in one of the large hotels on the seafront and James had insisted on escorting Emily.

'It will look odd if we don't arrive together,' he insisted. 'I'll pick you up in an hour's time.'

Emily would have preferred a milky drink and an early night, but the rest of the team was buoyed up and there was no way she could refuse to attend.

Molly Simpson's curtains twitched excitedly as James arrived at Emily's cottage exactly one hour later. Emily had been reluctantly forced into admitting he looked stunning in his evening suit and she battled with her nerves, as they were then obliged to open the proceedings by dancing a racy number together in front of everyone.

'Smile,' James's breath had tickled her ear as he whispered into her hair, 'and try to look as though you're enjoying the experience.'

'I am,' Emily countered back at him

doing her best not to grit her teeth.

Why did he have to look so jaw-droppingly handsome? It wasn't easy being indifferent to him.

James drew Emily's body close to his. 'That's a lovely shade of apricot pink you are wearing.' He adjusted one of her spaghetti straps that had slipped off her shoulder then twirled her round. 'Don't you think such a stunning dress deserves to be shown off under the spotlights?'

Emily's feet began to tap to the beat. Her parents were keen ballroom dancers and Emily had inherited their love of their favourite pastime.

'Everyone is looking at us,' James whispered in her ear.

'Then don't let me down,' Emily responded with a rustle of her skirts that drew an enthusiastic round of applause from the dining tables.

Coquettishly throwing back her head in a provocative gesture of invitation Emily went into the routine that had won her a junior silver cup.

James kept pace with her and Emily only realised the dance was over when a burst of applause signalled that the band had stopped playing.

Breathing heavily to thunderous applause Emily collapsed against James's chest. She could feel the rapid beating of his heart under her fingertips. Her own unsteady breath began to calm down and she sneaked a look at James from under her lowered eyelashes. It was not a wise move.

She stepped back instantly, wishing she hadn't been talked into buying the slinky silk dress from an extremely efficient sales assistant. It was nothing like the normal plain little black number she usually favoured on occasions like this.

'I'd better go and press some flesh,' James said as he gently released his hold on her.

'Yes, of course.' Trying to sound businesslike wasn't easy. 'I'd better do the same.'

'Another dance later perhaps?'

'I'm hoping to get an early night,' she replied.

If she had any more dances like that with James Bradshaw she knew she could be in serious danger of showing her feelings. It was vital she put as much space between them as possible.

'In that case I'll give you a lift home.'

'No, really,' Emily insisted. 'You stay and enjoy the party. I'll ease away quietly when no-one's looking.'

James tightened his jaw. 'As you wish,' he said and strode off in the direction of one of the corporate tables.

After doing the rounds of her own business contacts, Emily finally caught up with Toby and his friends and several familiar faces from the old West Hampton crowd.

'You can't leave, Em,' they insisted.

'Or are you too proud to play catch up with your friends now you're a local radio celebrity?' one of the lifeguards taunted. 'James Bradshaw is too grand to mix with us these days. Are you going to follow his example?'

After that remark there was no way Emily could leave the party early.

'So this is your idea of slipping away quietly is it?' James's lip had curled in an unpleasant twist as he witnessed her departure arm in arm with Toby and the last of the stragglers. They went out into the night air as the waiters were closing up the ballroom. 'I hope you're not driving,' he glared at Toby.

'Relax, James,' he assured him, 'we've ordered a taxi. I'll see Emily home safely.'

'I can see myself home,' she insisted, glad she had drunk no more than one obligatory glass of wine, but neither of the men was listening to her. They were glaring at each other like two stags at bay.

'See you do,' James warned Toby, 'otherwise you'll have me to answer to in the morning.'

★ ★ ★

Her insistent alarm bell going off what seemed like five minutes after she had

146

tumbled into bed shattered Emily's eardrums. She groaned and knocked it to the floor as she tried to switch it to mute. The only sound coming from the seafront was that made by the seagulls as they swooped along the promenade.

West Hampton was having a Sunday morning lie in. Emily wanted to stay in bed all day too and catch up on some much needed sleep, but her conscience pricked her. She needed to check up on the theatre and Sunday was a good day to catch up on her paperwork.

Correspondence levels had reached an all time peak after the article in The Herald. The reporter had gone totally over the top and cited a supernatural presence as being responsible for what had occurred in the old theatre wardrobe, along with quite a few exaggerated inaccuracies, all of which fuelled local interest. So far Emily had done no more than glance through a tiny proportion of the letters.

A supernatural society had also expressed interest in the phenomenon and wanted to run a workshop in the auditorium to see if they could sense any activity.

Emily wasn't too sure about that one, but the upside of all the publicity had been a gratifying increase in bookings after the ghost story had been run.

'Are you sure this was nothing more than a gigantic public relations stunt?' James queried the figures later when Emily had been forced to explain the reason for the upsurge in advance bookings.

James had appeared in her office as she was making herself a lunchtime cup of tea. Politeness forced her to offer him one as well and as he sat opposite her, looking incredibly refreshed after their late night, Emily couldn't shake off the feeling that he was checking up on her.

'We've already been through all that and the answer is still no.'

'Good because I can't have the security of The Alhambra jeopardised.'

'It wasn't.'

'If it was, for reasons of health and

safety I could close the theatre down.'

'You can't do that.' Emily flared up, spilling her tea over a pile of promotional leaflets.

While she dabbed at the mess with some tissues, James informed her calmly and with his most charming smile, 'I'm sure there's a clause somewhere in the small print that says I can.'

'You wouldn't dare.' Emily suppressed the urge to hurl her damp tissues at his pale blue cashmere sweater.

'Let me relieve you of those,' he said holding up the waste paper basket.

Peppering him with damp paper handkerchiefs would create exactly the right sort of opportunity James needed to invoke his wretched get-out clause Emily thought, as she watched him consign the rubbish into the bin.

'By the way, have you enough stamina left to go to Lottie's party tomorrow night?' he asked later in the afternoon as they finished running through the returns.

'Of course.'

Emily was pleased that after their initial spat she had acquitted herself quite well. Accounts were not her strong point, but James had been unable to find any faults in her bookkeeping and had been happy to sign off her figures.

'In that case can I give you a lift?'

'I'd rather make my own way, thank you.'

'I shall get a complex if you keep turning down my offers of a lift. It won't be any good relying on Toby to get you home this time. He lives at the farmhouse so he won't want to turn out to drive you back.'

'I wouldn't expect him too. I usually stay over at Lottie's after one of her parties.'

'In that case may I suggest you at least get an early night tonight?'

'James, I realise things looked bad last night but the old crowd know how to party. I hadn't seen them for ages and I couldn't let them think I'd grown away from them.' Their remarks about Emily becoming too grand for their company still stung. 'They've always been there for me when, well,' she shook herself. She had been about to say when her world was falling apart, but she couldn't let James know he had been part of the reason for her world disintegrating. 'Anyway, next thing I knew, it was late and the band had stopped playing.'

'I noticed,' James admitted with a wry smile.

'What were you doing skulking around the foyer anyway?'

'Waiting for you actually.'

'Why?' Emily demanded.

'I wanted to make sure you got home safely. You may not have over indulged but Toby looked a little jaded.'

'It may have escaped your notice, but I left with half the surf club as well as Toby and you could have joined us at our table. You didn't have to spy on me to find out what I was up to.'

'As you seem determined to refuse my offer of a lift, I'll see you at Lottie's party. Perhaps I can at least persuade you to spend some time with me there.'

Emily tried to concentrate after he left, but nothing she read seemed to make any sense and in the end she abandoned all pretence of work and went for a long walk along the cliff tops to clear her head.

She loved the view from Hampton Head; and, as she watched the evening lights twinkling in the harbour, she realised with a dull ache that the reason she reacted so violently to James Bradshaw was because, despite everything that had gone on between them, she was still in love with him.

★ ★ ★

The lane leading up to Pippins Farmhouse was clogged with cars and Emily was forced to park at the far end. She wasn't late but it looked as though the turnout was high and from the sounds of merriment drifting down the lane Emily was in no doubt that the party was already in full swing and promised to be one of Lottie's and Orlando's best. Emily picked her way across Lottie's lawn and inhaled the smell of newly mown grass.

It had been a long time since Emily had been to one of Lottie's parties. These days due to pressure of work her social life was minimal and she had grown out of the habit of wearing heeled sandals and a long skirt. Although the evening was mild she clutched her lilac pashmina around her shoulders in a gesture of self-protection. She was anxious to avoid sinking her heels into the damp grass or twisting her ankle down one of the numerous rabbit holes dotted about the garden.

Toby emerged from the marquee that had been especially erected on the lawn and strolled towards her.

'You look lovely.' He kissed Emily on the cheek as his eyes took in her sparkly top and black velvet skirt.

'So do you,' she complimented him.

Toby did indeed look heart-throbbingly handsome in his pristine white shirt, black bow tie and tailormade evening jacket.

'Had it made up for me at a friendly price by a man who's retired from the rag trade. He still likes to keep his hand in. Thought it might come in useful, you know, for premiers, the red carpet? Got to look my best.'

An impish smile dented Emily's cheek. 'Then we're honoured, Sir Toby.' She sketched a mock bow.

Toby grinned back at her enjoying the joke. Although he liked to play the peacock, at heart he wasn't vain and Emily suspected he didn't realise his handsome features caused many a teenage heart to go into overdrive.

'Come and have a drink, then I want to introduce you to Carly.

It had been a strategic marketing coup to engage the services of Carly Palermo for the summer season. She was the face of a range of cosmetics aimed at the younger end of the fashion market and this booking for the summer season was going to be her first foray into the acting world.

Media interest had been widespread creating yet more publicity for The Alhambra.

'I hope she isn't going to be too temperamental for us,' Emily voiced something that had been concerning her.

There had been references in the newspapers to artistic differences between Carly and her photographer boyfriend and these had also been cited as the reason for their very public split.

'Carly wants to make a new start in her career,' Toby replied earnestly. 'She's been taking acting lessons and had voice coaching. I've promised to give her all the help I can.'

'Do I detect something more than a professional interest in Ms Palermo's career?' Emily teased Toby.

He flushed and mumbled an explanation about only having just met and being good friends.

'Save that line for the tabloids,' Emily advised him.

'Look out,' Toby warned her, 'Lottie approaching stage right.'

Resplendent in yet another of her rainbow coloured silk dresses, with matching fascinator, Lottie headed towards them, arms outstretched in welcome.

'Darling, I had no idea you'd arrived. Toby, you naughty boy, why didn't you tell me the guest of honour was here?'

'Because I've only just stumbled on her myself,' he explained patiently.

Lottie linked arms with Emily. 'Come along. I've lots of people you simply must meet. Toby, make yourself scarce. That little girlfriend of yours was looking rather lonely when I spotted her by the water feature. Why don't you go and look after her?'

With a quick wave Toby headed off eagerly in the direction of the lake.

'Have you heard?' Lottie stage whispered, 'the naughty boy's now got a thing going for Carly Palermo?'

'He was telling me about it,' Emily replied.

'Hope it doesn't end in tears,' Lottie made a face.

'So do I,' Emily agreed, 'at least not before the end of the season.'

'Rehearsals for the summer show start next week don't they?'

Emily nodded.

'Well,' Lottie smiled at her, 'what do you think of my little party? I've pulled out all the stops and if this doesn't help convince James Bradshaw we are serious about The Alhambra, I don't know what will.'

'Thank you for all your help, Lottie. I don't know where we'd be without you.'

Lottie went rather red in the face and brushed aside Emily's thanks.

'Think nothing of it. I've been aching to get my teeth into a cause ever since I retired. You've no idea how dull retirement can be. By the way, a little policy of mine has just matured and I'd like to donate the proceeds to The Alhambra fund.'

'I couldn't possibly accept your policy cheque,' Emily protested.

'It's not for you, it's for the fund — to make amends,' Lottie insisted.

'Amends for what?'

Lottie turned rather red and glanced nervously over her shoulder. Clutching Emily's elbow she drew her away from the floodlights.

'I, er, well I haven't been entirely honest with you about certain matters. It's been playing terribly on my mind and when I told Landy what was worrying me he said I must confess.'

Emily felt fingers of apprehension creep up her spine. 'What do you mean?' she asked carefully.

'Landy would have nothing to do with my plan and neither would Toby but I couldn't let you struggle on alone. The only thing is I think I may have gone a little over the top.'

'Lottie, what have you done?'

'I only wanted to create some

publicity, you know, get the word onto the street, but that article in The Herald went a bit over the top, didn't it? I was only joking about a ghost.'

'Lottie.' Emily felt cold with shock and could hardly speak she was so angry, 'are you saying what I think you're saying?'

'I don't know, am I?' Her huge violet eyes widened in confusion.

'Was it you,' Emily asked, anxious to ensure there was no further misunderstanding, 'who broke into the wardrobe?'

'We've got a key, you see.' Lottie evaded a direct answer. 'Joe gave us one as honorary patrons and said we were welcome to visit any time we liked. I got the idea about Hamlet from an old theatre magazine. Of course I didn't realise it would take off in quite the way it did.'

Lottie's smile died as she took in the expression on Emily's face.

'That was an extremely stupid thing to do, Lottie.'

'I know, darling, I realise that now,

but I was only trying to help.'

'You do realise that apart from anything else, James Bradshaw thought it was me behind these tricks?'

'No.' Lottie's face was now a mask of horror and disbelief.

'He's also told me if there is any repetition he's going to close us down with immediate effect, and he means it.'

'He can't do that.' Lottie's guilt now turned to outrage.

'He can and he will. There's something in the small print that says so.'

'But all I did was resurrect that old story about a ghost haunting the Green Room. No-one really believed it. It was only a bit of fun. That's why I leaked the story to The Herald. It was a bit embarrassing when they rang me that day in the theatre when I was with you. Actually I thought you might have suspected then what I was up to.'

'A lot of people did believe the story, Lottie and I'm not sure what you've done isn't fraudulent.'

'Surely not,' she protested.

'And you are going to have to apologise personally to Ivy. She's extremely upset over what's happened and so too is Ted, and with due cause.'

'Of course, darling, I'll do anything I can to make amends.' Lottie sounded genuinely remorseful.

'Promise me there will be no repetition,' Emily insisted.

'Hand on heart, darling.' Lottie batted her eyelashes to full effect as she pleaded with Emily, 'But does James need to know it was me?'

'I think he's going to have to unless you want him blaming some other innocent person.'

'Emily. Found you at last.' A red-faced Orlando gasped her name as he crossed the lawn in a hurried trot. 'Phone call for you,' he tried to catch his breath. 'Took it in the kitchen.'

'What?'

'Emergency . . . '

What? Where?'

'Ted's been trying to get you on your mobile but said it was switched off.'

'What's happened now?' Emily demanded.

'Darling,' Lottie twittered, 'it's nothing to do with me, I promise. I've been here all day. Ask Landy.'

'Burst pipes, water everywhere. The theatre's flooded. Ted's called the fire brigade.'

'I've got to get back — now.'

Emily turned round and collided with the hard walled chest of James Bradshaw.

Another Disaster At
The Alhambra

'We'll take my car.' James grasped the seriousness of the situation in seconds and immediately took charge.

'There's no need for you to come with me.' Emily yanked her wrist out of his firm grip. 'I can deal with things. You stay and enjoy the party.'

She didn't want James breathing down her neck, suspecting another publicity stunt.

'Why do you persist in being so stubborn every time I offer you a lift?' he snapped.

'Because I can manage without your help.'

'This time you can't.'

'Why not?'

'For a start you are wearing totally

unsuitable shoes for driving.'

'All hands on deck,' Lottie's theatrically trained voice drowned out Emily's protest. 'Burst pipes at the theatre. Buckets, mops, bring anything you've got to hand and follow me.'

'We've got to get out of here,' James grabbed Emily's arm again, 'before that lot get going and totally block the lane.'

Hordes of confused partygoers were tumbling out of the refreshment tent, rushing around the garden looking for suitable receptacles, half of them not really sure what was going on, but all eager to join in.

'Come on,' James urged.

'Got to take my shoes off,' Emily gasped hopping around on one foot as her velvet skirt wrapped itself round her other ankle, 'can't run in heels.'

'For heaven's sake, darling, what is going on?' Toby appeared from the direction of the lake, hand in hand with Carly Palermo.

'Flood at the theatre. Ted's been on the phone.'

'What? I'm coming with you.'

James brushed aside Toby's offer of help. 'You'd be better seeing to that aunt of yours and stop her and her friends from making things worse.'

The situation on the lawn now looked as though it was getting out of control and while Toby hesitated, James seized his chance and dragged Emily down the drive.

'Can't keep up with you,' Emily gasped and winced as pebbles cut into the soles of her feet.

'You should have thought of that earlier and not worn such high heels,' James said showing little sympathy for her predicament.

'It's a party. What did you expect me to wear, lace-up brogues?'

'Want me to give you a fireman's lift?' James paused and made a movement towards her.

'No I do not,' Emily retaliated. 'You go and start your car.'

'Anything you say,' he replied with his slow smile, 'but if you don't catch up with me I'm leaving without you.'

'Brute,' she called after him as she splashed through a pothole.

Fuming, Emily barely had time to do up her seat belt before James began rolling his car forwards.

'How much did you hear of Lottie's confession?' Emily asked.

'Enough.' James narrowed his eyes in concentration as his tyres splashed through yet another puddle, 'and as far as I'm concerned Lottie Moulin is banned from The Alhambra forever,' he added.

'The flood is nothing to do with her.'

'It's banishment,' James insisted, 'or I invoke the health and safety clause.'

'Banishment will break her heart. She loves the theatre.'

'Stop sticking up for her.'

'I'm loyal to my friends and you shouldn't eavesdrop on private conversations.'

'Lottie caused havoc on my property. This time your loyalty is misplaced.'

Emily averted her eyes from James

and stared resolutely out of the windscreen. Privately she agreed with James, but there had been times in the past when Lottie had acted over and above the call of duty.

'Your decision,' James prompted.

'Is that your final word — banishment?' Emily asked in a quiet voice.

'It is.'

Emily felt sick. She knew she would have to accept it. If she didn't she had no doubt James would close the theatre down and everyone's hard work would have been for nothing.

James reached the end of Lottie's lane and swung out onto the West Hampton Road. Back on a hard surface, his car picked up speed and ate up the miles to West Hampton.

Emily's heart sank at the sight of the flashing blue lights circling the theatre forecourt.

'It looks like you won't have to invoke your wretched health and safety clause,' she grappled with her door handle. 'The budget will never stretch to having the old place redecorated. The wall hangings are Victorian and totally irreplaceable.'

'Sorry, sir.' An official signalled to them at the bottom of the hill. 'Can't let you go any further.'

'I'm the manager.' Emily leapt out of the car. 'I have to see what's happening.'

Still barefoot she sprinted up the hill.

She could hear James panting behind her. 'For heaven's sake put your shoes on.'

Emily grabbed them from him and thrust her feet into her ruined evening sandals.

'Ted,' she almost fell into the caretaker's arms as he appeared in the theatre doorway. 'What's happening?'

'It's the old lead piping in the kitchen around the back,' he explained. 'One of its joints burst. It's very weak in places and I suppose it's worn away with age. The damage isn't as bad as we first feared. Hello, sir,' Ted addressed James. 'I did my best but there was only me and Ivy on the premises and it took us a while to realise what was happening. By the time we did, the floor was waterlogged. I rang the emergency services after I turned the water off at the mains. They've pumped out most of the water but it will take a while to get things back to normal.'

'You did well,' James reassured him. 'Are we allowed inside?' he accosted a passing fireman.

'As long as you wear a hard hat and watch your footing. The structure of the building is sound, but the floor out the back is damaged and you can never tell what could happen with these old places. You'd better borrow a pair of our boots, miss,' the firemen looked at Emily's exposed toes. 'I can't let you inside without protective footwear.'

'I should never have gone to Lottie's party,' Emily apologised to Ted, 'I should have been here with you.'

'Nonsense. Ivy and me are fine and there's no-one like my Ivy in a crisis.' He nodded over to where his wife was busy dispensing mugs of tea from the urn they used on open days. 'Only took her five minutes to take control of the situation. We'll soon have the old place shipshape, you see.'

'No-one does anything,' James insisted, 'until I've seen the extent of the damage.'

'The stage area is fine, sir,' Ted replied. 'It's only out the back and we've got other facilities we can use if we need fresh water.'

'Then we could still open for the new production on schedule?' Emily's eager question tumbled from her lips.

'Don't see why not with a bit of give and take.'

'If I explain everything to the cast, I'm sure they'll understand. James,' she grasped his arm, 'any inconvenience would only be for a few days at most. Wouldn't it, Ted?'

'By my reckoning, that's about right,' Ted agreed with her.

'You can't close us down because of this mishap, James,' Emily pleaded with him. 'There's too much at stake.'

'It's not up to me. If the insurance company won't give us extra cover, then we won't be allowed to open.'

'We are already covered for flood damage, aren't we?' Emily demanded.

'They weren't best pleased about the business with the costumes. They agreed not to raise the premiums on the understanding there were to be no further claims for a period of six months.'

'You told them?' Emily echoed in disbelief.

'Of course I told them,' James snapped back at her. 'It would have been negligent of me not to.'

'But we didn't claim for anything. The costumes weren't damaged and strictly speaking there was no break in.'

'Are you coming to inspect the damage or are you going to stand here and try to think up more ways of arguing with me?'

Not giving her a chance to reply, James Bradshaw strode through the crowded foyer and down the back passage that led out into the small kitchen. The sight that met their eyes made Emily's heart sink. The floor was awash with bits of debris. Old programmes floated in the muddy water, along with cups, saucers and Ivy's container of cleaning fluids. The smell caught at the back of her throat and made her cough. Her eyes watered as she looked at James and wrinkled her nose.

'It's bad, isn't it?' she was forced to admit.

A reluctant smile tugged the corner of his mouth. 'I've seen worse. No need to give up the fight just yet. Ted's right. If we can pump out the worst of the water and clear up the debris the damage can probably be contained.'

Emily sagged against the wall in relief.

'Come on,' James moved towards her, 'it's not like you to give up without a fight and why aren't you arguing with me?'

Quite how it happened she didn't

know but the next moment James's arms were round her waist supporting her. She turned her face to his and his lips descended onto hers. Emily succumbed to his embrace even though every other fibre of her being was telling her that what she was doing was wrong.

Their hard hats clashed as James increased the pressure and when Emily finally broke free she was breathless and unable to speak.

'Goodness knows why but I've been wanting to do that for a long time,' James admitted, his eyes boring holes into hers.

Emily's mud spattered velvet skirt was now sodden and clung uncomfortably to her legs. The chief fire officer had found her a pair of industrial boots that were several sizes too big for her and the hard hat she was wearing had slipped down her forehead and was threatening to impede her vision. She blinked, trying to make some sense of the situation.

James snatched at his bow tie. 'I hate wearing these things,' he undid the knot.

Ted cleared his throat noisily and poked his head round the door.

'Tricia Longfellow's been on the phone,' he announced not looking Emily in the eye, 'with the station weather forecast for us. Seems we're due for a warm spell next week and she says it's going to last several days. So if we leave all the doors and windows open that should dry things out and help get rid of the smell.

'Soon as the emergency services give us the all clear, I'll organise a team of volunteers. I'm sure the sixth form college will be more than pleased to help out. Now their exams are over, all they do is hang round the seafront all day.'

'Thanks, Ted.' As well as his tie James had also undone the top button of his dress shirt and Emily's eyes were drawn to the pale triangle of flesh at the top of his neck. It was only with the greatest difficulty she managed to focus on what he was saying. 'I'll tackle the insurance. You'd better see what you can do to make the place habitable. We don't want the authorities coming down on us like a ton of bricks because we didn't follow correct procedures.'

'Hang on a minute,' Emily finished straightened her blouse that had become disarranged when James had kissed her. 'I make the decisions round here.'

Her elegant chignon carefully styled for the party had also worked its way loose under the pressure of her hard hat and she could feel a stray curl tickling the side of her face. She brushed it away with a quick flick of her fingers.

'Sorry, Em,' Ted stifled a laugh. 'I don't want to alarm you knowing how you feel about spiders, but I think you ought to know you've got one dangling from your left ear.'

'What?' she shrieked.

She froze as James leaned forward and very gently detached a piece of spider's web, with the spider still attached, from the side of her face.

'Give it to me, sir, I'm on my way outside. I'll find a nice quiet corner for it to get back to work.'

Emily did not notice Ted leave the kitchen.

'Are you sure you're all right?' James asked. 'You're looking pale.'

Standing opposite James in a flooded kitchen with the sounds of burly firemen tramping around in the theatre above them shouting orders to each other and Ted disposing of recalcitrant spiders was not the stuff of which romances were made, but the situation was as emotionally charged as if they had been lazing on a white sandy beach, surrounded by an azure blue sea and a sky dotted with white puff ball clouds.

'I'm fine,' Emily insisted in a hoarse voice. Her throat was sandpaper rough and it hurt to speak.

It was vital that she remember the logistics of the situation. James was her boss and if Emily didn't observe the terms of her contract and failed to produce results James would not hesitate to close the theatre down. It was as simple as that. What had happened between them was nothing more than an aberration, an accident of time.

'Emily, I,' James began.

She stepped backwards from him at the same time as a shadowy figure emerged from the darkness of the theatre.

'There you are, James.' Tricia Long-fellow bounded into the kitchen looking elegantly casual in her polo shirt and pedal pushers. 'Ugh,' she recoiled, 'what a disgusting mess.' She picked her way over a pile of damp rubbish.

'Why is it,' she laughed at Emily, 'every time we meet up you are wet and covered in sand or mud, or both? I really can't keep rescuing you from James, you know.'

She linked an arm proprietarily through his.

'Have you forgotten about the

interview you promised me?' she asked.

'No, I hadn't forgotten,' James replied slowly, making no effort to remove her arm from his but all the while keeping his eyes transfixed on Emily's.

Tricia widened her grey eyes innocently as she picked up on the taut atmosphere between the pair of them. 'Say did I interrupt anything here?'

Emily's reply was a clipped, 'nothing at all.'

'Are you sure? You only have to say the word and I'll make myself scarce. Ted's already offered me a bucket and brush and what girl could resist an offer like that?'

'We were inspecting the damage that's all,' Emily insisted.

'Not good,' Tricia agreed sympathetically. 'So, Emily, are you now going to admit defeat? I mean how can you keep The Alhambra going in the face of this latest setback?'

'I think,' James interposed swiftly, 'that Emily has enough to keep her occupied here without replying to any more of your questions, Tricia. We'd be delighted to conduct a radio interview with you at a more appropriate time, but meanwhile perhaps you could assure your listeners that The Alhambra is still standing and it's business as usual.'

Tricia shrugged. 'As you wish. The Alhambra means a lot to the people of West Hampton, James. I'm only doing my job keeping them posted of developments.'

'And we're very grateful to you.'

'Hey,' Tricia's face lit up, 'if there's nothing more you can do here, James, why don't I take you up on that interview now — down at headquarters?'

'I suppose there's no time like the present,' James agreed after a slight hesitation, 'and Ted seems to have everything in control here.'

'Great. Catch up with you later, Emily.'

Tricia cast a triumphant look over

her shoulder as, still linking arms with James and leaning closer against him than was strictly necessary, she carefully made her way out of the flooded kitchen.

Emily And James Discuss The Past

'Hope I'm not too late to order a drink with lots of ice.' Toby turned at the sound of Tricia's voice and smiled a greeting while continuing to polish the last of the lunchtime glasses. Her amber beads clacked against the bar top as she plonked her bag onto a spare stool and fanned herself with a bar menu.

'At least one bonus of this hot weather is that it should bring the tourists flocking down to West Hampton for the weekend.'

'Hope so,' Toby replied. 'Lemonade was it?'

'I thought you weren't working at the club any more. Or did I get that one wrong? I mean, now you're the face of West Hampton.' Tricia teased as she quoted from the article that had headlined in The Herald the previous week.

'I like to keep my hand in.' Toby placed the tea towel over the taps.

'So, how're things?' Tricia settled down on her bar stool and sipped the soft drink Toby had served her.

'I'm hard at work. It's better than resting.'

'The Herald liked what they saw of your performance at last week's preview.'

Toby did his best to look modest. 'They'll be singing someone else's praises next week I expect.'

'And Carly Palermo? How's she shaping up?'

Toby gave a self-conscious smile. 'You could say she's part of my increased workload.'

'I'm intrigued.' Tricia leaned forward and folded her arms on the bar. 'Tell me more.'

'Off the record?'

'Agreed,' Tricia nodded.

'Carly is finding acting harder work than modelling. She's mildly dyslexic and has difficulty learning her lines so rehearsals are a bit of a strain. Everyone is expecting so much of her. She knows the success of the theatre is riding on the summer season and the tension is beginning to tell. She's come out in a nervous rash and she keeps blanking even when I prompt her. She so doesn't want to let the production down by putting in a bad performance. I'm trying to help her but it isn't easy.'

'You do have a bit of a problem,' Tricia agreed. 'Poor kid. It can't be easy living in her famous father's shadow either. I know what it's like having a successful older relative.'

'To make matters worse Lottie keeps popping over to the studio when Carly and I are rehearsing. We thought getting away from the theatre would help, you know a change of atmosphere? But Lottie found out what we were up to and now she's forever dropping in and giving advice and well,' Toby shrugged, 'it's not always welcome.'

'I can imagine,' Tricia sympathised, 'she means well but it takes a while to get used to Lottie and then she is best taken in small doses.'

'I'm not saying Carly doesn't love her to bits, well,' Toby amended, 'maybe that's a bit of an exaggeration.'

'Their artistic temperaments clash?'

'Last night they had a bit of a set to. Lottie offered Carly some cream for her rash and began giving her tips on make-up. I mean Carly was the face of a make-up house.'

Tricia winced. 'Not very tactful.'

'Orlando and I had to calm things down. If Carly has many more days like that, I'm worried she might walk off.'

'Wish there was something I could do to help.'

'The trouble is there's nowhere else private we can rehearse. I can't really ask Lottie not to call in on us, I mean it is her studio and she lets me live there rent free.'

'Hey, you've given me an idea.' Tricia

said. 'I could offer you the use of my apartment. I live alone so you wouldn't be disturbed and no-one gets past the doorman without being vetted, so there's no danger of Lottie dropping in. Problem solved.'

'Don't you live in Harley's Point?'

'I do, in one of my uncle's properties.'

'I couldn't possibly afford the rent.'

'I'm not asking for money.' Tricia took another sip of her drink.

'You're not?' Toby looked puzzled.

'You and Carly are the answer to my problem. The thing is, I'm scheduled for a short holiday. You're welcome to make use of the facilities in my absence. In fact, you would be doing me a big favour. I don't really like leaving the place unoccupied while I'm away.'

'If you're sure?' Toby looked hopeful.

'I need someone to water the plants and air the place in this hot weather. So? Are you up for it?'

'That would be great,' Toby enthused. 'If you're absolutely certain you don't mind two theatricals having the run of the place?'

'Here's my spare key. I'll be back about the middle of next week, but feel free to come and go as you please. I'll leave word with the hall porter to expect you so there won't be any problem gaining admittance. Enjoy.' She flashed Toby a smile as she slid off the barstool and stood up.

'Thanks a million,' Toby smiled at her.

Tricia blew him a kiss. He watched her stride from the bar on the impossibly high heels that she liked to wear. Her rustic embroidered skirt floated around her slender figure and for a moment he regretted that there hadn't been more chemistry between them.

The sound of a customer clearing his throat drew Toby's attention away from Tricia and back to the bar.

'James, er, hello.'

He greeted the new arrival with a nervous smile and glanced swiftly towards the car park. To his relief Tricia had already driven off. Had James Bradshaw overheard them discussing him and the theatre? He hoped not, not that they'd done or said anything wrong, but he would feel easier in his mind if James hadn't seen the pair of them together.

'Toby,' he nodded a return greeting. 'I hope you're not overdoing things working here on your day off.' His voice matched the expression in his eyes.

'My days off are my own affair.' He tempered his reply with a polite smile. 'Wouldn't you say?'

'Emily needs to be able to rely on the support of everyone involved with the theatre to pull their weight. They can't do that if they're over-tired by other activities.'

'I'm well aware of that fact,' Toby made a big effort to keep his voice down. Arguing with a customer would not go down well with the management. 'Now is there anything else?'

James ordered a sandwich and

watched Toby prepare it.

'Was that Tricia Longfellow I saw leaving?' he asked.

'Yes. She's a member here and often drops in for a chat. Why?'

'You two seemed very friendly.'

'We are.' Toby garnished the cheese and tomato sandwich with some watercress and passed it over to James. 'If you'll excuse me I need to help clear the tables in the dining room.'

'Don't go without this.' James held up Tricia's distinctive key fob, displaying its brash Harley's Point logo. 'You'll need it to let yourself into Miss Longfellow's apartment.'

* * *

'I don't believe you and I don't listen to gossip.'

'Neither do I and this isn't gossip,' James insisted.

Emily had not wanted to accept his invitation to dinner. Ever since the night of the flood when he had kissed her, her thoughts had been in turmoil. Ted, whom she suspected had witnessed the scene, had persuaded her that it would be a good idea to have a night off and with Ivy urging her to go as well Emily had been unable to think of a suitable reason not to.

Facing James across the table at the latest fish bar to open on the sea front, Emily was annoyed with herself for agreeing to come. James hadn't wanted her company for the evening. He was using the pretence of a date to dish the dirt on Toby.

'I saw them together, Toby and Tricia at the club,' James insisted.

'I've seen you and Tricia together,' Emily pointed out, 'but I'm not inventing ridiculous stories about you and her and even if they were true they would be nothing to do with me. Now can we change the subject?'

'Tricia has given Toby the key to her apartment.'

'If you're so worried about it why don't you ask Toby what is going on?'

'I thought you might like to, seeing as you're closer to him than I am.'

Emily leaned forward. 'How many times do I have to tell you? Toby is his own man and what he gets up to in his spare time is no concern of mine.'

The waiter removed their untouched first course with a frown of concern.

'Is everything to your satisfaction, sir?' he asked James.

'Fine,' his eyes didn't leave Emily's face. 'Could you hold back the main course please?'

'As you wish.'

'I'm not hungry. Actually if you don't mind now you've had your say and told me about Toby, I think I'll leave.'

Emily would have pushed back her chair if James hadn't clamped her hand to the table with his.

'Please,' his voice was urgent, 'hear me out.'

'As far as I'm concerned I have, and if I stay here much longer and listen to you bad-mouthing Toby, I may be in

190

danger of . . . ' Emily looked round wildly.

'Doing something you might later regret?' James prompted with a smile.

Emily made a faint noise at the back of her throat.

'Then it's just as well you can't move without making a scene, isn't it?' His voice was soft and teasing as he increased the pressure on her hand. 'And in the interests of keeping the peace I'd say it's up to me to make sure you keep your dignity, wouldn't you? After all, these days you do have a social position to maintain in West Hampton.'

Emily's head was buzzing and she was finding it difficult to think straight. They were supposed to be having a disagreement. She wanted an excuse to argue with James. She didn't want him looking at her, the way he used to six long years ago in the days before she discovered how good he was at breaking female hearts.

'Talking of dignity, I've a confession

to make,' James confided.

'I don't want to hear it,' Emily insisted.

'Bad luck, because you are going to, then you'll know the sort of effect you have on me.'

'No, James,' she repeated, 'I don't want to hear it.'

'After Benito sacked me from my deckchair job,' he continued in a firm voice, 'I saw red, and if Lucy Jackson hadn't ripped up that silly bit of plasterboard I might possibly have crowned you with it. So there you have it. I'd say we're quits in the dignity stakes, wouldn't you?'

'Were you that angry?' Emily blinked at James.

'And some,' James admitted. 'It's not the experience of a lifetime to have your character assassinated in pink capitals for the whole world to see. Why didn't you give me a change to explain?'

'Can we talk about something else, please?' Emily asked.

'I suppose it was a long time ago,' he

conceded, 'and I probably was a bit full of myself that summer.'

Emily felt the constricting band tightening her chest ease a little. She breathed out gently.

'Yes, you were,' she said, determined not to go soft on James.

'But I didn't do half the things you accused me of,' he insisted.

Twin dimples dented her cheeks. She was beginning to enjoy herself.

'Benito believed them.'

'I hardly knew his niece.'

'She said she knew you.'

'Anyway,' James dismissed Benito's niece from the conversation, 'I'm sure we're both much better behaved these days.' He released Emily's hand.

Emily pushed back her chair and looked round for her bag.

'Yes, well, lovely as it is discussing the old days, I'm not in the mood to reminisce so, if you'll excuse me?'

'Where are you going?'

'Home, to heat up a tin of tomato soup.'

'Are you sure you won't stay here for dinner?' James coaxed. 'The chef's speciality tonight is lemon sole, catch of the day?'

Emily's stomach rumbled in response to his question. She knew there was a long waiting list for tables and James must have gone to a lot of trouble to get one.

'I bet you only had an apple for lunch.'

'I was too busy to take a proper break.'

'You always are. I remember you used to nibble apples in Benito's kiosk, didn't you, rather than take a lunch break?'

'It was our busiest time of day and the apples stopped me from eating too much ice cream,' Emily admitted.

'The first time I saw you, you were sitting on the seafront in one of my deckchairs nibbling at a red apple and reading a magazine.'

Emily had actually been using her magazine, as a cover to spy on James, but that was something she decided James did not need to know.

'Was it?' she shrugged nonchalantly. 'I really don't remember.'

She crossed her fingers under the table glad James had released her hand. She wasn't very good at fibbing and if James hadn't been gesturing to the hovering waiter to deliver their delayed main course, she suspected he might have realised how economical she was being with the truth.

'Why did you really come back to West Hampton?' Emily demanded.

Any faint hopes she might have entertained about James returning because of her were firmly quashed as he said, 'I read a write up on the resort in one of the Sunday supplements. I liked what I saw so I asked my agent to look out for a suitable property in the area. It came as a bit of a shock to learn that you were still here.'

'Why were you surprised?'

'I suppose I thought you would have moved on or followed Lucy's example and got married.'

'Working at the theatre involves unsocial hours and that's a death knell to any serious relationship.'

'It's the same in the property business,' James replied.

'Luckily my friends understand my commitment to my work. I can't count the number of parties I've missed, because by the time I get home I'm lucky if I can stay awake long enough to run a bath.'

'I hope you're still not thinking of rushing off tonight.'

The waiter approached their table and ground pepper over their lemon sole. Across the restaurant Emily caught a glimpse of Tricia Longfellow. She waved to James.

'I was actually,' Emily replied. 'It has been a busy week,' she affected a yawn, 'and I intend having an early night.'

She enjoyed the look of disappointment on James's face as she tucked into her lemon sole.

'Mmm,' Emily dabbed at her mouth

with her serviette, 'you're right, this lemon sole is delicious. Aren't you enjoying yours?'

The expression on James's face indicated that discussing lemon sole was the last thing on his mind.

Lottie Causes Further Upset

Lottie watched the ducks dive for food in the pond. She sighed loudly and rattled her teacup. Orlando frowned, recognised the signs of discontent and did his best to ignore them. Lottie poured herself a second cup of Earl Grey and sighed again. Orlando looked up from reading his newspaper and accepted the inevitable. Lottie was in one of her moods.

'What's wrong, old thing?' he asked with weary patience.

'Nothing.' Lottie's reply was tight lipped.

'Then could you please try to do nothing quietly?' he pleaded, 'I'm trying to concentrate on the reviews.'

'Reviews?' Lottie exploded, 'How can you read reviews at a time like this?'

'Is there something you want to talk about?' Orlando folded up his newspaper and tucked it down the side of his wicker chair.

'Don't let me interrupt your reading, please.'

Orlando helped himself to a second cup of tea and frowned at Lottie. 'Your trouble is, Lottie,' he pronounced, 'you are bored.' He sipped the hot liquid appreciatively.

'I am not,' Lottie contradicted him in a querulous tone.

'Why don't you do some gardening?' Orlando suggested. 'A spot of weeding might cheer you up.'

'I hate gardening and I hate the countryside.' Lottie swatted at a wasp. 'It's inhospitable, unfriendly and dangerous. I want to move. Landy, that wasp is out to sting me, do something.'

'You are out of sorts,' Orlando insisted, 'and that's why you're behaving like a spoilt child. You don't really want to move, you know that. You love living here.'

'How do you know I'm out of sorts?' Lottie demanded.

'We've been married long enough for me to recognise the tell tale signs.'

Lottie inspected her carefully manicured fingernails. 'It's Carly Polermo. What do you think of her?'

'She's a nice girl although her acting skills are sadly wanting.'

'You don't think she's got too much of a hold over Toby?'

'Possibly,' Orlando shrugged, 'but why don't we let Toby sort out his own life? He doesn't need us to interfere in his affairs.'

'That's just it,' Lottie admitted, 'I can't help interfering.'

Orlando raised his eyebrows. Experience had taught him that in these circumstances it was wise to say nothing.

'And I think this time I might have gone too far.' Lottie's face was an agony of uncertainty as she looked at Orlando.

'What have you done now?' Orlando demanded.

'I thought I ought to apologise to Carly, you know for that unfortunate scene over the face cream?'

'Go on.'

Lottie, picked at her cashmere shawl. 'She was in the studio on her own yesterday waiting for Toby to come back from his shift at the club.

'And?'

'I don't know how it happened. My apology turned into a rather heated exchange with Carly.'

'What about?'

'Amongst other things, her acting skills. We both said things that would have been better left unsaid. Toby arrived in the middle of it and came down heavily on Carly's side and told me that I was an interfering old busybody and exactly what I could do with my skin cream.'

Orlando buried his face in his spotted handkerchief as he did his best not to laugh. He could see Lottie was upset and the last thing he wanted to do was inflame the situation by seeing the funny side of the situation.

'He said they weren't going to stay here a moment longer and he took off with Carly and I've no idea where they've gone.'

Orlando turned his laughter into a cough. 'What can I say, Lottie? If you've really put your foot in it again, and I have to admit it does look like it, perhaps you ought to have a re-think about that little holiday I was suggesting?

'A change of scenery would do you the world of good. I could do with a break too. The Brittany coast can be lovely at this time of the year. What say we take off in the Bentley and do a bit of touring, visit our old haunts? Look up friends? We owe several people a visit and by the time we get back, things will probably have calmed down.'

Lottie chewed thoughtfully on her lower lip. 'You know James has banned me from going anywhere near the theatre during rehearsals?'

'Don't start on all that again,'

Orlando warned her.

'Because of James I haven't had a chance to speak to Emily for ages. She doesn't drop in so much now Toby's tied up with Carly. I do miss our little chats. I wonder if I could pop in on her at work? James need never know.'

'Don't even think about setting foot in the theatre,' Orlando looked alarmed.

'James Bradshaw doesn't scare me,' Lottie said with a robust toss of her head. 'You know, Landy, I really feel I've been treated very badly over this affair. I put in a lot of hard work promoting the theatre and all the thanks I got at the end of the day was banishment from James, and Toby telling me not to interfere. It's extremely upsetting and I can't say I'm not a little hurt.'

'It's my personal opinion you've been extremely lucky to get off so lightly.'

'I have been made a scapegoat. The reason James is so angry with me is because he's in love with Emily and he thinks I've upset her. That's the last thing I would do to the dear girl.'

Orlando gaped at Lottie. 'Now you are talking nonsense. Aren't you?' he asked uncertainly, unable to follow Lottie's logic.

'I am not,' Lottie insisted.

'But James and Emily don't like each other.'

'Indifference is the killer and no-one could say James and Emily are indifferent to each other. It's fireworks every time they meet up.'

'You know,' Orlando reminisced tuning out to Lottie's chatter, 'Emily showed a lot of courage with that pot of paint all those years ago. It wasn't very ladylike but it got the message across.'

Lottie waved a hand at Orlando. 'Landy, are you listening to me?'

'Yes, dear,' he answered automatically.

He had in fact been thinking that in matters of the heart, Lottie was rarely wrong and if she said James Bradshaw was in love with Emily Sinclair then the chances were she was probably right.

'I was saying, I've written to Emily.'

'Why?'

'I've sent her a cheque.'

'Lottie,' Orlando protested all thoughts of the strangeness of women swept aside, 'I wish you'd spoken to me first before making such a grand gesture. You know matters of finance are not one of your strong points. We're in a bit of a delicate situation with the bank. We've rather exceeded our limits. I received a stiff letter from the manager last week. We're going to have to rein in our spending for a while. You've been a mite extravagant lately, throwing parties and all the rest of it. We're not in a position to go splashing out on donations, much as we would like to.'

'It's all right,' Lottie reassured Orlando, 'the money was a bonus from a policy that matured last month.'

Lottie's smile was a little forced. She realised she probably shouldn't have added a little something extra to the policy pay out before she sealed the envelope.

'I hate having nothing to do,' Lottie complained. 'No-one's been to visit since the party. Ungrateful lot.'

'Which is where we came in, isn't it? Why don't we take off for a few days?' Orlando used his most persuasive voice.

'Could we book somewhere at short notice?'

'There's Bertie's cottage in La Baule. I could contact him and see if we could rent it out for a few days? It's been ages since we've been to Brittany. You could look up your old chums. You know how they love hearing what's happening on the scene here.'

'I wonder if they still serve those delicious crayfish at that little auberge we found along the coast. Landy, do you remember the lovely meal we had at the Coq d'Or?'

Orlando smiled at her glad to see Lottie was back to her normal self again.

More Problems At The Alhambra

'Have you heard the latest news,' Ted poked his head round the door to Emily's office, 'hot off the press?'

'Hmm?' Emily was only half listening.

'It's about Lottie,' he paused then enquired, 'is there a desk under all that paperwork?'

'Somewhere,' Emily replied. 'The stage curtains will fall apart soon unless they are replaced and they'll cost a fortune. After you've made dozens of phone calls to suppliers to try and get a good deal out of them it's difficult to keep up the charm. I'm beginning to wilt under the pressure.'

'You could try talking to St Vitus,' Ted suggested.

'Does he make curtains in his spare

time?' Emily asked.

'Not sure how handy he is with a sewing needle, but he is supposed to protect the acting profession from disaster.'

'Well, if you think it will do any good,' Emily smiled at him, 'feel free to give it a go.' She shuffled a pile of quotes into some form of order and pushed them to one side. 'What was that you were saying about Lottie?'

'She and Orlando have renewed their vows.'

Emily gaped at Ted. 'Really?'

'My informant tells me they're on honeymoon in France. Ivy is ecstatic. She loves a wedding, even a renewal. Says she's going to plan a big do for them when they return. Must get on.' Ted sauntered off leaving Emily still in shock over his news.

Emily wished she could check with Toby that the story was actually true but lately he seemed to be avoiding her. She hadn't spoken to him for days. She had left messages for him all over the place, but he hadn't replied to any of them and Emily was beginning to wonder if there was anything behind James's suspicions that he and Tricia Longfellow were up to something. Why else would he have the key to her flat?

But what was he doing there and where did Carly Palermo fit into the scene? She and Toby had been an item at Lottie's party, not Toby and Tricia. Although Toby and Tricia knew each other Emily had detected no chemistry between them and for all his faults, Emily couldn't see Toby breaking up with Carly quite that quickly. Even given Toby's standards that would be a tad swift.

Emily was reluctant to believe there might be some truth in James's veiled suggestion that Toby and Tricia might somehow be involved in one of Monty Smith's schemes, but it was a plausible theory and would explain Toby's behaviour and why he was staying out of her way. He would know that of all the people in West Hampton, Emily would be the most difficult person for him to deceive.

As well as being ignored by Toby, Emily had not heard anything from James after he had driven her home on the night of their dinner date over a week ago.

Miss Simpson's curtains had twitched as James had driven up to Emily's cottage. He had refused Emily's offer of a coffee and after a quick peck on the cheek that even the eagle-eyed Miss Simpson could not disapprove of, James had driven away. Emily knew she only had herself to blame for the coolness between them, but the end of the evening left her feeling flat.

As for Lottie, it was ages since she and Emily had spoken and Emily felt a twinge of guilt. After James had imposed his embargo on Lottie visiting the theatre, it had been difficult to find the time to drive out to Pippins, and as visits to Lottie were never an affair that could be rushed, Emily had been forced to let them drop.

The farmhouse was rarely unoccupied so even if Orlando and Lottie were on holiday Emily was sure there would be someone there to answer calls and keep an eye on the place. She dialled Lottie's number.

'Hello?' A breathless voice eventually picked up the receiver just as Emily was about to hang up after the call had rung out for several minutes. 'Pippins Farmhouse.'

'Is Lottie there please?'

''Fraid not.' The voice sounded uneasy.

'Mr Fawcett, Orlando, is he there then?'

'He's not here either.'

'Do you know when they will be back?'

'No, sorry, I don't.'

'Could I leave a message?'

'If you like.'

Emily frowned. 'That's not Manuela is it?'

'Er, what was it you wanted to say?' There was another uneasy pause.

'You're not the press are you?'

In the background Emily heard a male voice enquiring, 'Is that the taxi? Tell it to hurry up. We haven't got all day.'

She recognised the voice instantly. 'Toby? Was that Toby? Can I have a word with him?'

'Er, I don't think it is. I mean — hang on a minute.'

There followed a muffled exchange of conversation down the line.

'Look it's Emily Sinclair here,' she injected some crispness into her voice. 'I'm growing tired of this cloak and dagger stuff. If Toby is there I'd like to have a word with him, please.'

She heard more hurried murmuring in the background then jumped as the connection went dead. Emily stared at the receiver in disbelief as the dialling tone purred back at her. Toby, and she was sure now it had been his voice she had heard, had hung up on her. What was he playing at? And who was the female who answered the phone?

It rang again almost immediately. Emily snatched it up.

'What is going on?' she demanded.

'Emily?' a puzzled voice greeted her.

'Oh, hello, James.' Her voice reflected her disappointment.

'I have had more enthusiastic greetings,' he complained.

'Sorry, I was expecting someone else. What can I do for you?'

'You can prepare yourself for a shock.'

'Another one?'

'Has something happened?' James demanded.

'Ted's just told me Lottie and Orlando have renewed their wedding vows.'

'Good for her.' It was James's turn to sound disinterested.

'Is that all you can say?'

'Frankly, yes. Lottie is not my flavour of the month. Did you know that cheque she issued for the theatre fund has bounced due to insufficient funds?'

'What?'

'It's just as well we weren't relying on it to get us out of trouble, but I didn't call you to talk about Lottie. I've been in touch with the insurance company to update them on what's happening at the theatre and they are doubling the premiums on our policy.'

'Can they do that?' Emily clutched the receiver wondering how many more shocks she could deal with in one day.

'They can and they are, effective beginning of next month. Look, I need to speak to you,' James said, 'are you free for lunch?'

'I haven't really got time,' Emily began, annoyed that James should expect her to drop everything because he needed to talk to her.

'Make time.' The line went dead.

The receiver slipped from Emily's hand and fell back into the cradle. Her head was reeling from all that had happened in the space of an hour. What was so important that James had to see her immediately? She addressed her attention back to the curtains, and tried to see if there was a way she could square a better deal on the quotations she had received.

* * *

'It's not lunch time yet, is it?' Emily glanced at her watch as James burst into her office. As was usual when she was engrossed in her work, she lost track of time. 'My watch must have stopped. It says it's only half-past eleven.'

'Read that.' James tossed a letter onto her desk. 'It's from your leading lady.'

'Carly Palermo?' She picked up the piece of perfumed pink notepaper covered in Carly's flamboyant scrawl. 'Why is she writing to you?'

'It's her letter of resignation.'

'I don't understand.'

'She's leaving the summer show.' James spoke slowly and clearly. 'She's citing a panic attack. She's walked out.'

'She can't renege on her contract without giving notice.'

'Well unless you know how to track her down, there's very little we can do about it. As of now we are without a leading lady.'

A missing piece of the jigsaw clicked into place as Emily continued to stare at James.

'Say something,' he urged, 'before I explode.'

It had been Carly Palermo who had answered Emily's call to Lottie's telephone. That was why her voice had sounded so familiar. Emily hadn't spoken to her often but often enough to recognise her voice.

'I know where she is.' Emily jumped to her feet.

'What?'

'Come on. If we hurry we can stop her leaving and maybe talk her into changing her mind.'

'Where are we going?' James demanded.

'Lottie's farmhouse. She's with Toby.'

On The Hunt For Toby

Never had the drive from West Hampton out to Lottie's farmhouse taken so long. James drove as carefully as the winding lanes would allow, but their journey was hampered first by a learner who managed to stall his car at the West Hampton crossroads. Then after the way had cleared a tractor pulled out in front of them and took up the entire width of the lane, forcing them to stay back until it turned into a side field. As they passed it spattered James's car with clods of dry earth. Emily hardly noticed.

'Can't you go any faster?' she begged, her knuckles white as she gripped her seat belt.

'Not at the risk of losing my licence,' James replied calmly, 'and in case you hadn't noticed there's now a whole lot of hens running amok in front of us.'

Emily ran her fingers through her hair. It had been weeks since she'd had it trimmed and her neat shoulder length style was in danger of turning into a shaggy dog cut.

She always tried to look the part whenever they met up, but today James had caught her unprepared with his unscheduled burst into her office.

'Why didn't I guess something like this might happen?'

'Don't beat yourself up about it,' James still had his eyes on the road. 'You weren't to know and you can't nanny everyone.'

'Normally I try to stay out of production politics, but the office is not far from the stage and every day there were raised voices. I think Carly was in tears on one occasion.'

'I thought every production was like that,' James commented with a wry smile. 'It comes of putting too many fragile egos together in one place. I don't know how you stand it.'

'By the way,' Emily screwed up her nose. It hurt having to apologise to James. 'Thanks for not saying I told you so.'

'Not my style. Er, what exactly have I been so magnanimous about?' James queried lightly.

'Lottie's cheque.'

'The one that was returned unpaid?'

'I should have listened to you and not accepted it. The trouble is she doesn't bother reading things like bank statements.'

'Probably not and I agree with you. At times Dame Lottie inhabits a different planet to the rest of us and she does tend to leave everyone else to clear up the mess.'

The clucking of the hens outside grew more indignant.

'So she and Orlando have got married all over again?'

'According to Ted, yes,' Emily nodded. 'That's why she took off without telling anyone. I think after all that business over the ghost she invented, she needed to get away. Poor Lottie.'

'Why poor Lottie?' James frowned.

'You know how she loves any excuse to throw a party. There's no way she would have let an occasion as significant as renewing her vows pass unnoticed, but I suppose she finally realised the seriousness of what she had done.'

'We'll have to make it up to her when she gets back then, won't we?' James flashed Emily a smile.

'Have you forgiven her?' Emily was surprised.

'Shall we say there's a thaw in the atmosphere?' James admitted reluctantly. 'I never thought I'd say this, but I miss her.'

'Me too.'

'Looks like we're clear ahead.' James put his foot down on the accelerator and waved to the harassed woman still standing in the road clutching the last of her huffy hens to her chest.

'What are we going to do?' Emily

changed the subject, 'about Carly Palermo?'

'Maybe you could have a word with Toby and get him to use his influence to try to persuade her to stay on, if they're still at the farmhouse that is?'

'I could try but Toby can be quite selfish at times. If he's made up his mind to leave with Carly then I doubt anything I could say will make him change his mind.'

'Do you know what brought on Carly's panic attack?'

'She's not popular with the cast. Most of them think she only got this job because her father is Roger Palermo.'

'They were probably right.'

'I also gather she wasn't very good. People can be very forgiving if they think you're trying your best, but it seems Carly was playing the big star and demanding all sorts of rights.'

'Mmm, not good,' James agreed.

'I don't think anyone would be too bothered if her part was recast.'

'By the way,' James cast Emily a look. 'It's my turn to apologise.'

'What for?'

Why did James have to look so cool and in control, Emily thought, when their world was falling down around their ears? His shirt was fresh and newly ironed and his hair was neatly trimmed.

'About Toby and Tricia. There's nothing going on there. I bumped into Tricia by the lift at Harley's Point. Seems she offered Toby the keys to her apartment to use as a base while she was away on holiday. The story Tricia gave me was that Toby and Carly wanted to rehearse their lines together in privacy. They started off using Toby's studio, but Lottie kept barging in on them offering her professional advice and it wasn't well received.'

'Poor Lottie,' Emily said with a sympathetic smile. 'Seems she couldn't put a foot right anywhere. She was out of favour with you. Toby didn't want her interfering in his life and I wasn't allowed to speak to her.'

'That's not true,' James objected. 'I didn't want her creating any more behind-the-scenes havoc that's all.'

'Whatever, she used to telephone me all the time, but I haven't heard from her in ages.'

'At least Orlando didn't desert her.'

'He must be about the only good thing in her life at the moment,' Emily said.

'By the way, what was it you wanted to talk to me about over lunch?' she asked.

'It can wait,' James replied and began to slow down as they approached the lane leading to Lottie's farmhouse.

'Now before we go in all guns blazing you are absolutely sure it was Toby's voice you heard down the line this morning?'

'I'm sure,' Emily insisted, 'but what I don't understand is why he told Carly to put the phone down on me.'

'Something's not right,' James agreed as he swung the car his car through the gates of Lottie's drive.

Emily inhaled the scent of newly mown grass and realised with a shock they were almost halfway through the year. Lottie's beloved rhododendrons were in full bloom. The sun streamed across the lawn and Emily wished she had time to do nothing but bask in its warmth.

They drew up outside the farmhouse. It had the deserted air of an unoccupied property. James walked round to the passenger side of the car, opened Emily's door and waited patiently for her to get out.

'Thank you.'

She put her hand in his as she clambered out. It had been a long time since anyone had shown her such old fashioned courtesy. She knew a lot of men were scared of offending feminist principles and wary of making masculine gestures these days. Emily was glad James wasn't among them.

'Come on,' he urged, the tone of his voice dispelling her slight softening towards him. 'Let's try the main farmhouse first. If we get no luck there, we'll have a go at the studio.'

Emily pressed the bell more fiercely than she would have wished and tried not to glare at James as they faced each other on the doorstep while they waited for someone to answer their ring.

'What say we take next weekend off?' James suggested. 'A friend of mine has a boat moored in the marina, I'm sure he'd let us borrow it for the day.'

Emily blinked up at James not sure she had heard him correctly. 'Are you mad? I can't take a day off.'

'Yes you can and time away from everybody else would do you and them good. They'd have to sort out their own lives wouldn't they, and not come running to you every time something went wrong?'

'I'm the manager.'

'I need a break too,' James said, 'and I'd rather like to spend it with you. I'm only suggesting a day.'

'I'm not sure,' Emily stumbled over

her reply. 'I mean there's a lot happening at the moment.'

'Only a suggestion, but if you like I'll give you time to think up a better excuse than that. If you can't, we've got a date?'

The smile in his eyes suggested James was teasing as he turned his attention back to the door and tried to squint through the frosted glass. Emily tried not to notice the sun playing its usual trick on his hair, turning it golden like a modern day Greek god.

'Don't think anyone's in,' he said.

'James,' Emily grabbed out at his arm making him jump.

'What?'

'I've just remembered something else.' Emily recalled what had originally alerted her to the sound of his voice in the background. 'Toby asked if I was the taxi.'

'Well,' James looked round, 'if they ordered one,' he spied car tracks in the drive, 'it looks like it's been and gone. Any idea where?'

'None at all.'

'I don't think anyone's going to answer the bell here, do you? It's probably pointless but we'd better check out the studio.'

Their feet made crunching noises as they walked over the pebbled pathway towards the studio.

A flash of sunshine on glass at the end of the drive caught Emily's attention. She looked away from James to where a familiar classic three litre Bentley was bowling towards them.

Lottie was in the passenger seat and wearing an outrageous concoction of feathers and lace on her head. She was waving enthusiastically and Orlando seated beside her raised his panama hat as he brought the car to a halt.

Lottie began flapping her fingers in the air before Orlando had time to open her passenger door.

'Landy, open the door, there's an angel. Don't hang about doing nothing. I want to show Emily my lovely new wedding ring.' Lottie held up her left hand and flashed her third finger at Emily. A white gold band sparkled in the sunshine. 'You've heard our news, I suppose?' she called over. 'We wanted to keep it quiet but you know how it is. My publicist leaked it to an acquaintance and the next thing we knew it was all over the net — so tiresome.'

Lottie's annoyance would have been more convincing if she hadn't been smiling broadly at Emily.

'Lottie, shut up, old thing and let me get a word in edgewise,' Orlando chided her. 'Emily, my dear, how lovely to see you.'

Lottie put her hand in Orlando's and with all the dignity of her theatrical training emerged from the car.

'James, hello dear. I do hope we're friends again. I've got so much to tell the pair of you.' She air-kissed him then turning to Emily hugged her. 'You're shockingly thin. What on earth have you been doing to her, James? Overworking her I suppose. Well I won't have it. Landy, get some of that lovely French cheese and the wine out of the boot. We'll have an early lunch while we catch up on all the news. Now come along, you two,' she linked her arms through theirs. 'You can start by telling me everything that's been going on while we've been away.'

'Lottie,' Emily tried to protest, 'it's lovely to see you again but I don't think we've got time for one of your lunches.'

'Nonsense,' Lottie insisted. 'If I don't feed you you'll only nibble on an apple and you can't think straight on an empty stomach.'

Emily cast an imploring look at James just as his mobile phone began to ring. He walked away from her to take the call.

The End Of The Little Alhambra

'Toby sent you a text?' Emily realised it was futile to resist Lottie's offer of lunch and hoping to keep the meal as short as possible helped herself to some of Lottie's creamy French cheese. She refused Orlando's offer of wine, opting instead for mineral water.

She, Lottie and James were seated on the terrace while Orlando bustled round filling up glasses and setting out plates of nibbles for everyone to eat.

'It's important in times of trial to keep up your strength,' he insisted, agreeing with Lottie as he opened a tub of glistening green olives.

'Yes, it was the day before yesterday,' Lottie answered Emily's question. 'That's when we decided we had to come back. Landy, give Emily some of that lovely bread to go with her Camembert, but for goodness sake don't saw at it like that, it's not a tree trunk. Oh and some black grapes would be nice. Sorry we haven't got any apples, darling, I know you like those crisp red ones. James, some cheese for you as well?'

'Toby's text?' Emily prompted as James looking up from his mobile phone refused Lottie's offer of anything to eat. Another call came through and he wandered away from the table.

'What? Oh, yes. Sorry, getting confused in all the excitement. Toby said Carly was threatening a nervous breakdown. That dreadful rash finished the poor girl off and she wanted out. Toby said they were going to go away together to sort things out and he'd be in touch and that I wasn't to worry about him. That's about as much as I can tell you.'

'I can't believe Toby would leave us in the lurch,' Emily shook her head still unable to come to terms with what he had done.

'You know actors,' Orlando cut in, 'crazy, the whole bunch of them. That's why we enjoyed the life, didn't we Lottie?'

'I never let anyone down.' Lottie adjusted her headdress that had slipped slightly in all the excitement. 'Toby's behaviour is outrageous, totally unprofessional and I shan't hesitate to tell him so next time I see him.'

'I thought the production meant so much to him.' Emily still could not quite believe Toby had deserted them. 'It could have been his big chance.'

'I think, well, maybe there were other things on his mind.' Lottie swallowed a grape thoughtfully.

'Such as?' Emily queried.

'Insider knowledge.' Orlando tapped the side of his nose, a knowing look on his face.

James strolled back to the table having finished his call. 'Sorry, Emily, more bad news. I don't know how to tell you this, but the summer show may have to fold.'

Emily pushed away her plate of cheese. Her appetite had deserted her.

'What do you mean?'

'I've been in touch with the backers.'

'You didn't waste any time telling them about Carly.'

Emily could feel the cheese she had just eaten churning in her stomach. How she could even have contemplated a day sailing with James was beyond her. He had already written the theatre off as a lost cause and was probably busy negotiating a new deal on another property. That's what all the mobile phone activity had been about.

James shook his head.

'They were in touch this morning before I even knew about her and Toby. That's what I wanted to talk to you about. They are experiencing financial problems and now they say they are not prepared to go ahead without a name.' He shrugged. 'Sorry. They've pulled out.'

'This is what you've always wanted, isn't it?' Emily's hazel eyes crashed into his. She knew she was being unfair but she couldn't help herself.

'That's not true,' James voiced a gentle protest. 'I gave you nine months and if it's possible to get the finance together I still intend to stick to my part of the deal.'

Emily wanted to believe him but with so much loaded against them she wasn't sure about anything any more.

'Let's not be too hasty about things.' Orlando's interruption injected some calm into the situation. 'Lottie and I have been in this position several times before and it isn't always the end of the line. Things might not be as bad as they seem. You know,' he joked, 'the darkest hour always falls before dawn.'

'How can you say things may not be as bad as they seem?' Emily turned on Orlando. 'Did you know Lottie's cheque has bounced due to insufficient funds?'

'Sorry, darling.' Lottie looked stricken. 'I wouldn't have had that happen for the world.'

'The insurance company has increased our premiums. The latest production looks like being pulled and the leading man has run off with the leading lady because she can't cope with the pressure. How bad does it need to be?'

James gave Emily's fingers a sympathetic squeeze. 'We're all upset,' he reminded her quietly, 'no need to fly off the handle at poor old Orlando. None of this is his fault, or Lottie's come to that.'

A wave of shame swept over Emily. 'Sorry, Orlando, Lottie,' she apologised, biting her lip, immediately regretting her outburst. 'I didn't mean to sound off at you.'

'Sound away, my dear. My shoulders are broad enough to take it. I won't be offended by anything you say,' Orlando smiled at her.

'And that goes for me too,' Lottie put in. 'Plain talking never did anyone any harm and compared to some of the actresses we've worked with your outburst was a model of restraint. Now what we need is an angel,' Lottie spoke calmly, 'Do you know anyone, Landy?'

'Already racking my brains, old girl.'

Emily stood up. 'You've both been so kind and supportive. All the same I think if you don't mind, I'd better get back to the theatre. I rushed out without telling anyone where I was going. Everyone will be beginning to wonder what's going on and if the story breaks about Toby and Carly, I'd rather I was there to explain exactly what has happened.'

Orlando rose to his feet. 'I understand completely and don't worry, Emily, Lottie and I will put our heads together and try to come up with something.'

James and Emily walked back to the car in silence. Emily, still ashamed of her outburst, didn't know what to say and James seemed preoccupied with his own thoughts. There were no hold ups on the drive back to the theatre and he dropped her in Alhambra Place about ten minutes later.

'Are you coming in with me?' she asked.

'Sorry, I've an important appointment. I'll be in touch later.'

He drove off as Emily was trying to thank him for the lift. She bit down on her anger. There was no point in getting further stressed out. James would be eager to get his new deal on the road and now she was no longer of any use to him he wouldn't see the need to hang around. So much for his fine words about always being there for her, Emily thought.

'It's bad news,' Emily greeted Ted after she'd walked up the hill to the theatre.

'So I hear.'

'You know?' She looked into his kindly concerned face.

'You can't keep a thing like that quiet in a place like this,' Ted explained. 'The wires started buzzing soon after you left. One of the crew got a call from an agent asking if the stories she'd heard were true. Rumours were flying around about the backer pulling out and the possible collapse of the production. Everyone's been released for the day. Did you manage to find out what was going on?'

Emily shook her head. 'Toby and Carly have disappeared. We don't know exactly where they are, but we don't think they're coming back. Lottie and Orlando arrived while James and I were up at the farmhouse, but they're as much in the dark as the rest of us. I feel I've let everyone down. Ivy must be devastated.'

'Don't go blaming yourself. You couldn't have done any more or worked harder. Now Ivy's busy brewing up gallons of tea, get yourself a cup then come and tell us what you do know. Nearly everyone has stayed on to hear what you've got to say and to offer you support. Want me to get the troops on stage?'

Emily nodded. She was touched by the cast's loyalty, but at the same time she dreaded the prospect of officially breaking the bad news.

'I'd better get it over with sooner rather than later.'

★ ★ ★

Emily sat in the deserted stalls. It didn't worry her being alone in the theatre. In accordance with the best traditions of their profession, the cast had left the ghost light illuminated in the centre of the stage even though their world was falling down around them. Emily watched it flickering in the darkness its light a brave beacon of hope.

Hushed groups had made their way quietly out of the theatre, most of them heading for the wine bar after Emily had made her announcement about all that had happened.

She couldn't help wondering about James and where he was. She swallowed down her bitter disappointment over his desertion when she needed him most. They had stood side by side on the stage at Joe's leaving party because he had wanted to present a united front yet he hadn't stayed around when things started to fall apart. Emily didn't think it was possible to feel so sad.

Joe Sykes would be devastated too, thought Emily. After all the faith he had placed in her, she hadn't been able to save his theatre.

In the office she heard the telephone ring more than once, but she wasn't up to issuing a press statement and she had nothing to add to the rumours. She supposed James would make his intentions known once he had formalised the situation, until then she was as much in the dark as everyone else.

A supportive group of cast members had huddled around Emily after she made her speech. No-one blamed her for what had happened which had only served to make Emily feel more wretched.

'Hello? Anybody there?' A voice echoed down the aisle and Emily smelt a waft of French perfume.

She turned at the sound of footsteps

and saw Tricia Longfellow striding towards her.

'How are you?'

'You've heard the news?' Emily watched Tricia sit down in the next seat.

'I think everyone in town knows by now. I'm really sorry, Emily. If there's anything I can do?'

'Thanks,' Emily's smile was on the shaky side.

'I suspected something of the sort might happen when Toby told me of his plans.'

'Toby told you what he was going to do?' Emily repeated in surprise.

'We had a mini conference in my apartment a couple of nights ago. You know I leant him the key? He was using my place as a bolthole.'

Emily nodded.

'I tried to persuade him not to do anything foolish but without success. He'd read something addressed to Lottie. It was supposed to be a confidential email, but Lottie had given him her password to gain access to her correspondence while she was away, so of course he opened it. It was all there about the backers and the problems they were having. He swore me to secrecy, Emily. I wanted to tell you, but I couldn't.'

'It doesn't matter now.' The tiredness of the past weeks was beginning to catch up with Emily. She closed her eyes wearily and leaned back in her seat.

Tricia cleared her throat. 'If you like,' she paused then said, 'I could have a word with my uncle.'

'No,' Emily sat bolt upright.

'I think he's gone off the idea of developing the land surrounding the theatre. I was talking to him about it the other day. He realises the importance The Alhambra holds in the structure of the town and I think he'd like to be a part of it.'

'Sorry, Tricia, I don't mean to be rude, but involving your uncle would only be putting off the inevitable. If we're going to close, it's best we do it now. I don't want to raise everyone's hopes only to have them dashed again. Thanks for the offer,' she added hastily, 'it was a kind thought.'

'Well the offer's open ended if you're interested.' She smiled. 'What's James got to say about things?'

'He hasn't said anything much really. We drove up to Pippins to see if we could stop Toby from leaving but the farmhouse was deserted. While we were there Lottie and Orlando arrived back from their honeymoon. They cut short their holiday when they heard the news. They're as devastated as everyone else.'

'James must be devastated too.'

'No, he isn't,' Emily tilted her chin at Tricia. 'He's got what he wanted. He's already putting another deal together.'

'Not with my uncle he isn't, and you're wrong about James you know,' Tricia smiled. 'He was right behind the theatre's success and you.'

'Where on earth did you get that idea?'

'Instinct.'

'Well this time it's let you down.'

'I don't think so. I admit I set my cap at James when he first arrived in West Hampton, but he was, shall we say, unresponsive? Every time I tried to get close, he backed off. In the end I suspected there was someone else and the only person it can be is you.'

Emily was glad that in the darkness of the stalls Tricia could not see her blush.

'Like everyone else I heard about the paint incident on the seafront. You don't do something like that unless feelings are running high.'

'I was only nineteen and I thought I was in love with him,' Emily admitted with a shamefaced smile. 'I was wrong.'

'But you are now?' Tricia asked in a gentle voice, 'in love with James?'

'No,' Emily dismissed her suggestion. 'I got it wrong this time as well. Clearly my feminine instinct is not so finely honed as yours.'

They lapsed into silence for a few moments.

'You know,' Tricia was the first to speak as they looked round the faded theatre, 'this is exactly the place to fall in love, isn't it?'

'In a haunted auditorium?' Emily looked at Tricia in surprise.

'It's steeped in romance. Everyone who was anyone played here. Those autographed photos in the corridor bear testament to that. There must have been loads of love affairs hatched in the wings. In its day it had a glamorous image. It played host to all the big names of the day. People turned to The Alhambra for comfort and to forget their troubles.'

'You'd make a great public relations officer.' Emily's sadness softened as she listened to Tricia. 'Sorry I can't offer you the job.'

'Well, any time there's a vacancy, I'm your girl. Now I suppose you don't feel like joining the others in the wine bar? I'm sure we'll find most of the cast there and it won't do us any good moping around here on our own.'

'You go on ahead and if I feel more sociable later I'll catch you up.'

'Make sure you do otherwise I'll be sending out a search party.'

A throbbing sensation in the pocket of her jeans alerted Emily to an incoming call on her mobile phone. Half expecting it to be James she bit down a feeling of disappointment as Lottie's name flashed up. Emily switched her phone to divert. Whatever Lottie had to say would wait.

She knew she should really try to get hold of James before she spoke to anyone but she was beginning to wonder now if she would ever see him again. How could she have been so wrong about him? Twice. Wearily she got to her feet. As soon as this was all over she would take off and pay a visit to her parents in Minorca. She needed to get as far away from James Bradshaw as she could.

'I Had Never Really Forgotten You'

The sky was an intricate tapestry of lemon and purple and faded blue. Where it merged with the sea the colour turned a deep shade of vermilion. The bandstand with its filigree pillars, ornate in the dying sunlight and silhouetted against the encroaching night, stood quietly dignified against the burgeoning night sky. Emily sighed. As sunsets went West Hampton had pulled out all the stops.

She felt James stir beside her and wondered if his thoughts were running along the same lines as hers.

'If I close my eyes I can almost hear the brass band playing one of their military marches,' Emily said overcome with nostalgia as she leaned over the railings inhaling the salt spray of the ebbing tide as it moistened the night air. She took several deep breaths to slow down her racing heartbeat.

'Don't remind me,' James shuddered.

Emily turned to him in surprise. 'Didn't you enjoy the Sunday afternoon concerts?'

'I enjoyed the music itself, but you haven't lived until you've erected one hundred recalcitrant deckchairs and placed them in a semi circle around the bandstand. They nearly all blew inside out whether it was windy or not and I nearly lost the tips of my fingers on more than one occasion.'

'Poor you,' Emily sympathised.

She hadn't realised she had placed her hand on his arm. Her unconscious gesture caused a flare of an emotion in James's eyes that could still threaten to set her pulses racing despite all they'd been through.

'You got the easy end of the deal in your snug little kiosk.'

The temptation to retaliate to that remark was too strong for Emily to resist.

'Now there you're wrong. Life wasn't exactly easy in the ice cream parlour,' she pointed out, 'especially when the pump thing decided to throw a wobbly.'

'Point taken.' The expression on James's face set Emily's stomach on a crash course in somersaulting. 'Still there were happy days weren't they?'

It was no good. She had done her best to ignore the chemistry between them. There were so many reasons to dislike James, real and imagined. No matter the circumstances, she was as much in love with him as she had been six long years ago, but now with the impending closure of the theatre, James would be moving on and it was time to say goodbye again, this time forever.

James's mouth softened and Emily felt him relax as they listened to the sound of the sea lapping the sand.

'In those days we could afford to be happy,' she said. 'We had no real responsibilities apart from supervising deckchairs and ice cream cones.'

'And in the evening there was always

a beach party to go to. You kept in touch with some of the old gang?'

'Through Toby yes.'

His name hung in the air between them.

'Toby,' James echoed. 'We always seem to come back to Toby.'

'He has played a significant part in my life.'

'Will you miss him now he's with Carly?'

'I don't suppose this latest relationship will last any longer than the others. It's a bit more intense that's all.'

'Then you haven't heard the news?'

'What news?' Emily asked.

'I caught the local headlines as I was leaving. They're married.'

'Toby and Carly are married?' James flinched as she raised her voice. 'Sorry,' Emily apologised, 'I didn't mean to shout, but are you sure?'

'Is that so surprising?'

'It's priceless. I never thought he would settle down.'

James continued to look puzzled by

her reaction. 'Aren't you heartbroken?'

'Far from it. Toby loves to be the centre of attention far too much for us ever to have been an item. I suspect Carly likes the limelight too. I think they could be in for a stormy ride together.' She laughed to herself. 'Can't wait to hear Lottie's take on the marriage.'

'Well I'm glad you're not too upset.' James looked relieved. 'I must admit I was surprised when I heard the news.' He cleared his throat. 'I always thought he would ask you to marry him.'

'He did, once or twice'

Emily enjoyed seeing the reaction in James's eyes. For a moment she could almost have convinced herself he was jealous.

'What made you turn him down?' he demanded.

'I could never take him seriously,' Emily replied. 'Toby was fun to be with, but that as far as things ever went.' She paused, 'but you didn't only suggest this meeting to talk about Toby did you?'

Emily had been about to close up the theatre for the evening and head home to her cottage when James's call had come through. Her first instinct had been to turn down his invitation but she was glad now common sense had prevailed. She and James needed to talk and if she had gone home for an early night, sleep would have eluded her.

'Let's walk along a bit,' James suggested. 'That's if you don't want to join the others in the wine bar?'

Emily shook her head. 'I told Tricia I might catch up with everyone later but it was a polite excuse.'

'Me too.'

Keeping a respectable distance between herself and James in order to avoid any accidental touching of hands Emily allowed herself to enjoy the early evening. It was her favourite time of day in West Hampton.

The fishing fleet was moored, the traders had closed up and the visitors had returned to their hotels and boarding houses for dinner. The seagulls too had departed the scene. At this time of day the seafront was a haven of solitude. Without the smell of frying fish and the constant patter of the sea front traders it took on a more dignified air.

'So you've seen Tricia?' Emily tried to ignore the senseless stab of disappointment piercing her chest. It looked as though Tricia had also been economical with the truth when she said she hadn't been in touch with James.

'She sent me a text,' James replied, 'but it's not Tricia I want to talk about either. It's us.'

James paused as if uncertain how to continue. As Emily waited for him to speak she noticed the dark circles under his eyes

'You looked tired,' she sympathised in a gentle voice. Being tired was something she knew all about lately.

'I have been burning the midnight oil.' James blinked his sandy eyelashes several times as he stifled a yawn.

They had by now reached the end of the promenade and Emily realised to her horror they were standing close by the entrance to the old boathouse. It was where James had first kissed her, but the memory still lingered and she could tell by the expression in James's eyes that he remembered too.

'You know my work has taken me all over the world, but there's no place like West Hampton.'

'I find that hard to believe.'

'It worked its magic on me from the moment I arrived. It was old fashioned but honest and respectable and the people were friendly.'

'And you want to repay them by selling off one of the town's prized assets?' Emily found it difficult to keep the bitterness out of her voice.

'No, I don't. I bought into West Hampton because I wanted to be part of the scene.'

'That's not how West Hampton sees it.'

'And what about you?'

'Me?'

'How do you see my presence here?'

Emily shrugged. 'Without the theatre I don't really have a say in anything any more but I would hate to see West Hampton go the way of its neighbours.'

'That's why you were on your guard against me from the word go, wasn't it?

'Did you expect anything else?'

'Not really. I was the enemy, wasn't I? I didn't want to be, but I knew you'd never believe me if I told you I had the theatre's best interests at heart.'

'Sorry, I don't follow,' Emily frowned.

'It's difficult to explain. I don't really understand it myself, but I hadn't been back at West Hampton for five minutes before I realised I was fighting a lost cause.'

'James, I'm not sure what you're talking about.'

'I'm talking about us.'

'Then I'd rather you didn't say any more on the subject. Our past has nothing to do with the present and we have more important issues to discuss.'

'I don't think so and I'm not talking about the past. I'm talking about the future, our future.'

'James, don't.' Emily bit her lip. 'It's late, perhaps we can postpone this talk until a more suitable time? Perhaps when we're not feeling quite so drained?'

'When I saw you on that stage at Joe's retirement party glaring daggers at me it was as if the years had rolled away. I was so pleased to see you but you were looking at me as if I was the hound from hell. I wanted to laugh out loud at the expression on your face.'

'You could hardly have expected me to greet your arrival with any degree of warmth.'

'No, I didn't expect that,' James agreed.

'Did you realise I was the manager of the theatre before you bought it?' Emily asked.

'Not at first,' James replied, 'but when Joe started talking about his manager I realised who you were.'

'And you didn't want me out of the deal?'

'Not at all. I thought it would be a good idea if I pretended I wanted to develop the land surrounding the theatre.'

'Why?'

'I counted on you staying on, if only to try and get the better of me and I was right, wasn't I?'

'You mean it wasn't a business decision to buy the theatre?'

'Yes and no.'

'Nobody buys a theatre on a whim.'

'You're right, but I thought I'd wing it and see. You see I had never really forgotten you. Maybe our timing hadn't been right in the past, but even after six years I couldn't get you out of my mind.'

'Why didn't you tell me any of this earlier?' Emily demanded. Her throat was now so dry she could hardly speak.

'I didn't think you would believe me and I did try to on several occasions,' James admitted with a wry smile, 'but every time I saw you, we ended up having words or dealing with disasters, or being interrupted by dotty actresses or ex-boyfriends. It was as if fate contrived to keep us apart.'

'I've told you Toby was never my boyfriend.'

'You always looked very close to me.'

The evening had now grown chilly. James was wearing a black polo necked sweater but his body felt warm against Emily's as he put out a hand and caressed her gently under the chin. She twisted her head away.

'No, James, don't.'

'Why not?' he persisted.

'I can't.'

'Are you saying you don't feel the same way about me?'

'Yes. No. I don't know.'

James was so close to Emily now she could almost feel the stubble on his chin. Emily held up her hands and planted them on James's chest in an attempt to keep him at bay. He put his hands on top of hers and underneath her fingertips she could feel the steady rhythmic beating of his heart.

'I have no idea where my life is going.'

James now circled her wrist with his fingers. His voice sounded as hoarse as hers as he said, 'Don't you want us to be together?'

'I'm not sure I could ever trust you again.'

'Why not?'

'I don't have to give a reason,' Emily insisted.

'I think you do.'

'You can't just sail back into my life and expect me to drop everything because you want to rekindle our relationship.'

'How do you want to play it then?' he demanded.

'James, please don't.'

She was breathing hard now. She wanted James to kiss her, but she knew if he did there would be no turning back.

'You do believe me about Lucy Jackson, don't you?'

'It doesn't matter. Lucy is the past.

We have to move on.'

'Don't be too hasty,' James began, but his words were interrupted by Emily's mobile phone. 'Don't answer it,' he said.

'I have to. It may be important.'

'Darling, where have you been?' Lottie's voice floated down the line.

Emily heard James mutter under his breath as he moved away from her.

'I've been trying to contact you for hours.'

'Sorry, Lottie. I've had one or two things to attend to.'

'Well, whatever you are doing, stop it immediately because I have news. I'll see you in the wine bar in five minutes.'

James's figure was a darkened silhouette in the twilight. He had turned his back on Emily as she took the call from Lottie.

'I have to go,' she said. 'Lottie's got something to tell me.'

She saw James nod his head. 'Of course.'

'Will I see you tomorrow?'

'Perhaps,' James replied, 'I'll be in touch.'

She watched him stride back along the promenade and wished with all her heart she had followed his advice and not taken the call from Lottie.

A Change Of Fortune For
The Theatre

'Tiffany Snow?' Emily frowned at Lottie, fearing she had misheard. After her sleepless night nothing Lottie was telling her this morning made any sense whatsoever.

'That's right, darling.' She beamed at her. 'Isn't it wonderful news?'

'What's Tiffany Snow got to do with Toby?' The heavy feeling behind Emily's eyes was turning into a serious headache.

'Nothing at all.'

'But you said their names were linked.'

'I was talking about Tiffany Snow taking over from Carly Palermo. Darling, do try and keep up.'

'I'm doing my best,' Emily put a

hand to her forehead 'but can you please explain things in words of one syllable?'

'No stopping Lottie when she's on a roll,' Ted murmured from the pit.

'I should have known from the moment I first saw the poor little thing, I'm talking about Carly Palermo now,' Lottie added with a glance at Emily, 'that she wouldn't fit in. She was wearing yellow. No wonder she came out in a rash.' Lottie shuddered. 'Bad news or what? I mean anyone with the slightest savvy knows you do not wear yellow. It's almost as bad as clapping backstage.'

'I thought green was unlucky,' Ted emerged from the pit, wiping his hands on a dirty rag.

'And yellow.' Lottie fixed him with a beady stare.

Emily spoke carefully. 'Toby and Carly are definitely not coming back?'

'No they're not and if I wasn't such a lady,' Lottie went off at a tangent again, 'I'd say what I really think of Carly

Palermo and Toby too.'

'Thought she had been holding forth on the subject for the last half-hour,' a member of the cast muttered.

Landy breezed into the auditorium a beaming smile on his face. 'Morning everyone. All raring to go?'

'I mean, she quoted from The Scottish play and you can't get much more unprofessional than that, can you?'

'Right, well can we please get this meeting back on track?' Emily raised her voice. Members of the cast were beginning to grow restless and Emily sympathised with them.

'What we need to know, Em,' someone spoke up, 'is do we still have a job?'

'Of course,' Lottie interrupted. 'Isn't that what I've been saying?'

'Has Tiffany Snow really agreed to take part in our summer production?' Emily demanded.

'Don't forget Max Lloyd,' Orlando put in. 'We've got him as well.'

'Yes, that divine young husband of hers too.' Lottie placed a hand on her chest. 'I tell you, Emily, his career is in the ascendancy. Tiffany Snow and Max Lloyd are the golden couple of the moment and my clever Landy has managed to persuade them to star in our little production.'

A smattering of applause broke out from the cast. Emily turned to Orlando hoping she might get some sense out of him. 'Are you absolutely sure about this?'

'Hand on heart, my dear. It seems Max has got an aunt in the area who's not been feeling quite the ticket and they are planning to pay her an extended visit while she convalesces,' Orlando explained.

'Cherry Maltravers. Might have known she'd get in on the act,' Lottie snorted.

Orlando lowered his voice as he spoke to Emily, 'Lottie's feeling a bit put out. Cherry was, well, not to put too fine a point on it, an old flame of mine. Before I met my darling Lottie, of course. Anyway when I explained our little predicament to her, she said Max and Tiffany are resting at the moment and that she was sure they would be more than willing to help out. She got onto their agent immediately and it's all in the bag. He phoned this morning to confirm.'

Until then Emily could not shake off the feeling that Lottie was being over theatrical.

'Nice one, Orlando,' one of the stagehands called over, 'we owe you big time.'

'Yes, come on everyone, back to work before we all get star struck. The show must go on.' The stage assistant did his best to assemble those present into some form of order. 'OK with you, Em? You finished up here?'

'For the moment,' she nodded, 'and thank you everybody for staying on.'

'That's what the business is all about, isn't it?' someone called back. 'Sticking together in times of stress.'

'Lottie,' Emily demanded when the

cast began to drift off, 'who is this angel you were talking about?'

'No idea, darling.'

'We need to talk,' Emily insisted and drew her away from the confusion surrounding the stage.

'I'll stay out front and keep an eye on things here.' Orlando waved at them. He settled down in one of the stalls and opened a newspaper.

'I tried to keep the lid on it until I had a chance to talk to you personally last night, but I was bursting with excitement and I'm afraid I was a little indiscreet,' Lottie twittered as Emily shepherded her into the relative quiet of the back office. 'When you weren't at the wine bar with the others,' she shrugged her slender shoulders, 'my excitement got the better of me and I let it all out. Darling, I'm so sorry, but it's your fault, you know. You should have been there. Where were you?'

Emily decided it was in no-one's best interest to inform Lottie she had at the time been taking an evening stroll along the seafront with James Bradshaw. The rumour machine was in serious danger of crashing from information overload as it was.

'You weren't answering your messages and then when I finally got through to you, Landy received a last minute call from his agent for a live guest appearance in a chat show. Someone had dropped out and we had to high tail off to London at short notice. Too frustrating for words. Did you have an early night? You don't look as though you slept a wink.'

Emily's head had not cleared after her restless night going over and over what James had told her about still being in love with her. Or had he? Had he actually said he loved her? Emily wasn't sure.

'I didn't get much sleep,' she admitted.

'Why don't you go home? I could answer the telephone for you and take messages?' Lottie suggested.

'Lottie, I don't want to go home.

What I want are some sensible answers from you. Now sit down and start from the beginning.'

Lottie pouted. 'Darling, there is no need to be quite so brisk. I'm doing my best but I'm so excited. I'm sorry if I'm not making much sense.'

Emily took a deep breath to control her patience as Lottie fussed about the place, dusting imaginary dirt off the spare chair.

After Emily had taken Lottie's call by the boathouse she had headed for the wine bar only to find everyone in a state of chaos and confusion with no sign of Lottie or Orlando.

'They were looking for you,' Tricia explained. 'Something about an angel? What's that?'

'A backer, a person who puts up money to help a production.'

'I may have got it wrong. Lottie was on a bit of a high, but I think she's found one.'

'I need to speak to her.'

All Emily's attempts to track her

down had proved fruitless and in the end Emily had returned to her cottage too exhausted to do anything more than to crash out in bed. Sleep had evaded her until the sky was streaked vermilion, then she had fallen into such a deep sleep her alarm had failed to wake her. She had been late arriving at the theatre and missed the first part of Lottie's speech.

'What happened was,' Lottie took a deep breath. 'Sorry, darling, I need to steady myself. I am absolutely hopeless at explaining things.' She adjusted her glasses as they again slipped down her nose. 'I need to get my story absolutely right. James would expect nothing less of me.'

Emily drummed her fingers on the desk. Lottie liked to take her time, but time was a commodity in short supply. Emily glanced at her watch. Where was James?

Lottie was speaking again and Emily struggled to concentrate on what she was saying. She could think about

James later when she had all the facts about the rescue deal to hand.

'After all that happened yesterday Landy and I decided to go through our address book. You know, give it one more chance? That's how he came across Cherry Maltravers' name. Anyway, we were thinking maybe we could set up a consortium to help out. I know joint ventures aren't always a good idea, far too many people want to have their say in how things should be run, but when you're desperate you'll try anything.'

For all her air headedness, Lottie had a shrewd head on her shoulders and Emily could see the logic of what she and Orlando had been trying to do.

'Go on.'

'The trouble is, people move around so much and half the folk on our list weren't on the numbers we had. Usual stuff, they'd moved on, or changed partners, or if we did manage to speak to them they'd gone and got themselves in a financial fix and while they would love to help, maybe another time? It was pretty disheartening I can tell you. Sorry, darling,' she caught the expression on Emily's face, 'I am getting to the point. Landy and I had more or less come to the end of our list when Tiffany Snow's agent rang.

'Cherry had mentioned our problem to him and he came up with a possible solution. Did I mention he's an old friend of mine? Anyway we had a lovely long talk about the old days and then he said he was sure there was a benevolent fund or something that helped out in these kinds of circumstances.'

'It's the first I've heard of it,' Emily said.

'Me too,' Lottie agreed, 'Although it's not unusual for people to make bequests to that sort of thing.'

'You'd better give me the details,' Emily grabbed up a notepad, 'I'll check them out.'

'That's it,' Lottie raised her arms, 'we don't have them.'

Emily's shoulders sagged. She should

have known better than to listen to Lottie's outrageous tale of a last minute recovery.

'So it's all moonshine?'

'No. The money's there, we checked.'

Emily frowned. 'I'm not sure I like the sound of this, Lottie. What money?'

'Exactly. My suspicions were aroused too. Landy got onto the bank immediately, he's got the private number of the financial chap who looks after our affairs and he said he was about to call us because a large credit had just gone through and these days they have to be careful about things like that. He wanted to know all about it and did we need his financial advice? Landy told him it was already ear-marked and could we have the money immediately? He said he didn't see a problem and that was that.'

'Lottie, this isn't another elaborate scheme of yours?' Emily asked.

'You can check it out yourself. I've written down all the details.' She began to search in her capacious handbag before producing an envelope. 'Here it is, the agent's number and the name of the bank contact. I've also provided Landy's account details for your information. I've told the bank you'll be calling and that you have our authority to ask any questions you like.'

Emily stared at the slip of paper Lottie had thrust into her hand.

'And James doesn't know about this or does he?'

'I haven't seen him,' Lottie arched an eyebrow, 'but a little bird informs me the real reason you were incommunicado last night was because you and he were enjoying a stroll together down on the seafront?'

'How did you find out?' Emily gasped, then bit her lip. Caught unawares she had walked neatly into Lottie's trap.

'Gosh, you do look guilty.' Lottie patted Emily's hand. 'There's no need, I think it's perfectly lovely.'

'Lottie, please,' Emily implored, 'I'd rather you didn't say anything to anyone, about anything.'

'As if I would.' Lottie put a finger to her lips. 'But I've got to say I knew it would come right between you in the end.'

'This benevolent fund,' Emily steered the conversation away from herself and James and tapped the piece of paper Lottie had given her, 'I'll have to check things out.'

'Of course. Everything's there.'

'And Orlando really has been in touch with Tiffany Snow and Max Lloyd?'

'Hand on heart, darling. Isn't it too thrilling?'

'Isn't our production a little provincial for them? I mean they are used to commanding huge fees.'

'Not a problem. Tiffany's part has been written out of her soap at her request because there's a film deal in the offing but nothing's been finalised and Max is in more or less the same position. They are both available and have expressed an interest in keeping their hand in with some real live acting. For once, darling, everything is working in our favour. So when do we roll?'

'We don't until I've cleared things with James.'

'Well hurry up and clear them then.'

'And do I have your absolute promise that you will do nothing to interfere with the summer show?'

Lottie blinked at Emily from behind her purple-framed spectacles.

'Greasepaint flows in my veins, darling. I love the theatre, even if the old place is in need of some tender loving care.' She indicated the shabby walls of the office and the peeling paint on the window ledge. 'I give you my word that if Hamlet should appear it will be nothing to do with me. There does that satisfy you?'

'Thank you, Lottie.'

As Lottie bustled happily out of the office the telephone began to ring.

'Emily?' James's voice crackled down the line. 'Bad signal. How are you?'

'Fine. Listen, James, I've got some

news. Can you come down to the theatre now?

'Been called away. Can you hold the fort until I get back?'

'James, about last night and what you said about us,' she began then looked up to see Lottie creeping into the office.

'Forgot my bag. Don't mind me,' she mouthed in an exaggerated whisper before tiptoeing back out, quietly closing her office door behind her. Emily's heart sank. It would have to be Lottie who overheard her telephone conversation with James.

'Sorry. I spoke out of turn. I won't mention the past again.'

'No, James I . . . '

'Look I've got to go.'

'James,' Emily called down the line, 'we've raised some new finance for the summer production.'

'Good news.' His voice faded again.

'And we've also engaged Tiffany Snow and Max Lloyd to take on the two leading parts.'

'Who are they?' James's voice began breaking up.

'Don't you watch television?'

'Not often. Can you deal with it until I get back?'

'If you're sure you want me to.'

There was a crackly pause before she thought she heard James say, 'break a leg,'

'You too,' Emily added softly, but James had already rung off.

The Truth Comes Out

Emily stifled her third yawn in as many minutes. 'I may never move again,' she murmured a dreamy look creeping over her face.

'Suits me.' James's voice was warm in her ear as they sat side by side in the Oriental garden, enjoying the late evening air. Party noises drifted through from the theatre, punctuated by the frequent popping of champagne corks.

The sky was a patchwork of colour that showed no sign of fading for the night.

'I don't think it's going to ever get dark. Look at that sun. Talk about a last curtain call. It doesn't want to leave the stage either.'

Its dying rays cast a beam of light on Emily's chestnut hair.

'Congratulations,' James said for pulling it all together.'

This was the first time they had been alone together after their night walk along the seafront. James's business interests had kept him away from the area and it was only for the last ten days that he had been back in West Hampton and a physical presence in Emily's life.

She hadn't realised how much she had come to rely on him and it was an emotion she didn't know how to deal with.

'Everyone did their bit,' she replied, 'it was a team effort.'

'I'm sorry I wasn't here to help you more, but I did check the finances behind the deal and I was in touch with Lottie and Orlando's bank.'

Emily stifled an urge to rest her head on James's shoulder and drift into sleep against the warmth of his body. Tempting though the idea was there was still too much emotional baggage between them for such an intimate gesture.

Would James honour his agreement

about the theatre now they had found added finance? Whatever happened, Emily knew her future was still uncharted territory.

She was beginning to regret her impulsive gesture when she had turned James down saying they had no future together. He had promised not to mention it again and he hadn't.

Emily caught a glimpse of her old employer sharing a joke with Orlando as Maisie nattered to Ivy. She waved across to them. 'I'm so glad Joe and Maisie made it to the party. Joe looks about ten years younger, doesn't he? I haven't really had a chance to speak to him. Perhaps I should go and have a word.'

'You can catch up later,' James insisted. 'You're dead on your feet. Anyway aren't there other things you would rather discuss?'

'What sort of things?' Emily stifled another lazy yawn and decided to risk nestling up to James. Her eyelids began to droop.

'Are you listening to me?' James asked with exaggerated patience as her lashes fluttered in an attempt to keep her eyes open.

'Sorry?' Emily tried to hide another yawn. 'I think I'm in danger of crashing out. What were you saying?'

'Obviously my seduction technique could do with a bit of refinement.'

'Is that what you are trying to do, seduce me?'

'At the risk of being accused of going over old ground I'm trying to talk about us. I was hoping that during my absence you might have had a rethink?'

'Has anyone mentioned you have very nice eyes?' Emily smiled sleepily.

'My mother might have once or twice,' James admitted with a slow smile, 'but I don't mind you having a go as well if you want to.'

'You'll get big-headed if I do. Why don't you return the compliment about me?'

'All right,' James looked thoughtful,

'your hair is the colour of,' he hesitated, 'conkers. Is that any good?'

'Not very,' Emily shook her head. 'One of my old boyfriends used to say it reminded him of shiny chestnuts.'

'Did he? Well it may surprise you to learn that I don't want to hear about any of your old boyfriends and if you are giving me the green light on getting personal together I'd rather we do it somewhere more private. There are too many distractions here. How soon do you think we can leave?'

'Not for hours. I'm the hostess. In fact I should be circulating, not sitting outside with you.'

'I thought you might say something like that,' James replied with a resigned look on his face.

'Where is everybody?' Emily looked round. 'You'd think more of them would be enjoying the evening air instead of being crammed inside The Green Room.'

'I've bribed them to stay away from us while we talk.'

'You've done what?' Emily's heart missed a beat.

'It seemed a good idea. I can never get you on your own.'

Emily stared at him, lost for words.

'Are you certain we couldn't leave Lottie in charge and sneak away? I'm sure she wouldn't mind. She's in her element and she seems to know everyone here.'

Emily found her voice. 'I'm surprised at you for suggesting such a thing,' she managed to gasp.

'Are you?'

Emily could feel the heat from James's body as he leaned in towards her.

Over the past ten days an intimacy had grown up between her and James. It was an intimacy born of necessity.

'We carry no passengers,' Ted insisted the first time James returned to the theatre after his business trip.

A paintbrush had been thrust into his hand as he caught sight of Emily holding a torch and crawling around on all fours helping Max Lloyd look for one of Tiffany's dropped contact lenses.

'The trees need a freshen up. Nice and green. Off you go. You can talk to Emily later.'

Night after night they shared take-aways in the stalls with the rest of the cast while chaos reigned around them.

'Is it always like this?' James asked as yet another business update was interrupted while he clutched a torn costume and Emily did a running repair to the seam.

'It's not normally this quiet,' Emily responded, as there was a resounding crash from backstage. James half rose to go and offer some help. 'Leave it,' she advised him.

'Four large pepperoni, three medium cheese and tomato, one olive,' a delivery boy called down the aisle.

'Here,' James grabbed one of the boxes. 'Quick,' he nudged Emily as he opened it.

A fragrant smell of pepper and tomato wafted out.

'Have some before the gannets backstage scoff the lot.'

'Careful, don't spill cheese on the costume.'

It was all Emily could do not to dribble as James fed her a morsel of pizza.

The first time James had linked fingers with hers and squeezed encouragement when he thought the others weren't looking, Emily's stomach had done a cartwheel.

The second time he did it and when it was obvious the gesture was spotted by an eagle-eyed member of the cast who proceeded to make ostentatious attempts to slip away, Emily had been obliged to stifle her laughter as the poor culprit became entrapped in a stage prop that someone had left lying around and came crashing to the ground almost at James's feet.

Emily had tried to convince herself that the hand holding gestures were no more than tokens of support, nevertheless they always left her feeling hot and unsettled and the victim of knowing smiles from the technicians and anyone else who happened to be hanging around at the time.

'You know,' Emily recalled, 'I don't think I'll ever get over seeing you swaying up a ladder clutching a screwdriver in your teeth with a roll of sticking tape in your hand, while Tiffany Snow was on stage underneath you, sporting a hard hat and gamely rehearsing her dance routine.'

'One for the scrapbooks,' James agreed.

'Wish I'd had my camera with me.'

'Thank heavens you didn't and thank goodness the scenery behaved itself tonight. I wouldn't like to put my handiwork to the test for the whole season.'

'If it hadn't, Tiffany would have taken it in her stride.'

'She's a sport isn't she?'

'She and Max were brilliant.'

'They may even convert me to day-time television,' James acknowledged.

Tiffany Snow had sparkled as the ingénue playing alongside her husband as the handsome devil-may-care lead. Their enthusiasm infected the rest of the cast and that night everyone had given the performance of their lives.

'I think we've got a success on our hands,' Emily replied.

'By the way, did I see Toby lurking around in the wings?'

'Poor Toby,' Emily's face softened. 'He's here with Carly and her father.'

'Don't waste your sympathy on him.'

'I've never seen him so subdued. I'm not sure how he's going to take to married life.'

'That's his problem.'

'You don't sound very sympathetic.'

'I'm not, neither am I going to waste time talking about him.'

'Marvellous turn out.' Orlando ambled out of the Green Room and into the Chinese Garden. 'I know you gave us strict instructions not to play goose-berry, James, but you both look as though you could do with a bit more refreshment. May I top you up before supplies run out? That lot in there are drinking the stuff like it's going out of fashion.'

He replenished their glasses with a flourish.

'There, that's better. Enjoy. I'll now make myself scarce. By the way, the local delicatessen has just delivered a tray of hot lasagne if you're interested. Nibbles are all very well, but they don't fill a hole in the stomach do they?' Orlando waggled his bushy eyebrows at Emily. 'And I bet you've eaten nothing but apples all day.'

'Thank you, Orlando.' Emily stood up and kissed him on the cheek, 'for everything.'

'Not at all, my dear, my pleasure.' He hugged her back. 'I say,' he delivered his best roguish smile, 'being kissed by the most beautiful girl here really will get Lottie going. Is she looking our way?'

'She is,' James confirmed, 'although she's pretending not to.'

'Better get back then. Goodness me,'

he said as more cars began driving up the hill, 'people can't still be arriving. If things carry on like this we'll have to continue the party on the seafront.'

'Any chance of Emily and I leaving early?' James suggested to Orlando. 'Emily's half dead on her feet and I can't remember the last time we worked a less than eighteen-hour day.'

'Of course, dear boy.' Orlando winked at Emily. 'You go home, my dear. Don't worry about a thing. Lottie's got enough adrenalin to keep the show on the road for hours. I've never seen her on better form.'

Orlando ambled back to the action calling out greetings to everyone he passed.

'I take back all I said about Lottie and Orlando,' James said. 'They have been brilliant. I promise never to ban Lottie from the theatre again.'

'I can't believe you did that,' Emily protested.

'Did what?' James asked, a wary look in his eye.

'Asked Orlando's permission to leave the party. I can make my own decision when I want to leave and I told you I can't leave early with you.'

'That's an awful lot of leaves,' James didn't look as though he was taking her seriously, 'and why can't you leave?' he asked.

'Just because.' Emily ran out of argument.

'You're not still worried about a little gossip are you? Most of the people involved in the production have done nothing but talk about us for the last ten days. They've got nothing new left to say.'

Emily looked to where the latest arrivals were busy crowding round Orlando. One of the figures looked disturbingly familiar. She had never met him but she had seen his picture many times in the financial pages.

'What's the matter?' James asked picking up on her frown.

'Is this your doing?' she demanded.

James looked to where Emily was pointing.

'You mean Monty Smith? I had no idea he was coming.'

Monty raised his glass towards them.

'What's he doing here?' her eyes narrowed.

'I expect he came with Tricia.'

'He's a gatecrasher.'

'There's no need to get worked up about it. I'm sure he'll behave himself and he's one of the few people here wearing a jacket and tie.'

Emily slumped back down against the wrought iron back of her seat slightly ashamed of her outburst.

'Sorry. You're right I am over-tired. I only have to see Monty Smith to start imagining he is up to something.'

'Come on,' James urged, 'let's go. Orlando will make our apologies.'

'I suppose it would be all right,' Emily stood up slowly and stretched her aching limbs.

'Sorry to butt in.'

It was Tricia who now hovered hesitantly by their bench, her grey eyes troubled. 'I know this isn't the best moment, but Uncle Monty and Lottie's ex-husband are having a bit of a set to.'

'You said he would behave himself,' Emily turned on James.

'Joe and Orlando are doing their best to calm things down.'

The sound of raised voices reached their ears.

'What's it all about?' Emily asked.

'I'm sure it's something they can sort it out without my help,' James had now stood up too and was hustling Emily towards the garden gate.

'It's to do with the consortium.'

'The consortium?' Emily echoed, 'you mean Lottie's financial package?'

'Lottie's ex is insisting he's the main benefactor.'

'He probably is,' Emily replied, 'he was the one who told her about it in the first place.'

'I know, but Roger Palermo and Uncle Monty say they put up the major share. You'd better come and sort it out, James, before things get out of control.'

'What's it got to do with James?' Emily asked her suspicions aroused.

She had been too busy to give much thought to the rescue package, but it had been niggling at the back of her mind. Lottie was vague on details and Orlando had been reluctant to discuss it as well.

'It was James and Uncle Monty who proposed the idea of a consortium,' Tricia's voice faded as the enormity of what she had said began to sink in.

Emily looked from Tricia to James then back to Tricia again.

'Are you saying your uncle is involved in the theatre rescue plan?' The question scorched Emily's throat. 'And that it was James who set it up?'

Tricia raised a hand to her mouth a look of horror on her face.

'James, I'm so sorry. I thought Emily knew.'

'Emily, listen,' James began.

'I've wasted enough time listening to you.' Emily shook his hand off her arm. 'You're one of these people who cannot tell truth from fiction, aren't you?'

'No I . . . '

'Don't worry.' Emily knew her smile was a nasty sneer scarring her face but she was so angry she didn't care. She didn't think it was possible to hurt so much. 'I haven't got a tin of pink paint to hand, so I'm not about to go public on this one. Besides, I don't think there's a sheet of plasterboard big enough for me to state exactly what I feel about you.'

'Emily,' James called after her, 'where are you going?'

'You can have your theatre,' she flung the words back at him. 'You can do with it what you like. I resign.'

A Heartfelt Explanation

'I know you're home. Emily, answer the door.' Emily could hear James bellowing through the letterbox as he thundered on the knocker. She ducked down under her bedroom windowsill, hoping he hadn't spotted movement behind the curtains.

Why hadn't she thought to tell Molly Simpson last night that she was taking a short holiday to visit her parents in Minorca and to deal with all visitors? Her neighbour was certain to be peering through her nets to see exactly what was going on. James was making enough noise to wake the dead.

Ignoring the urge to shout at James to go away, Emily held her breath. She had no wish to ever speak to James

Bradshaw again. Neither did she have any intention of answering the door.

As far as she was concerned she and James were finished. He and Tricia Longfellow were welcome to each other. They were two of a kind and she hoped they would be very happy together devastating wildlife and scarring the countryside with their heartless development.

She heard footsteps receding down the cobblestone hill and breathed out in relief. If she was quick she had time to pack a shoulder bag with a few essentials and make for the airport. Her mother would lend her anything she needed once she arrived on the island, and right now Minorca was the only place she wanted to be.

She still could not believe James's treachery. He had promised her nine months in which to turn the theatre's fortunes around. When things had gone wrong he had turned to Monty Smith for help, something he had promised not to do.

Obviously he was more of a business-man than she had realised and money counted for everything, more than the lives of the people he had ruined.

She suspected that now he had a foot in the door, Monty Smith would buy James out and that would be that. The Chinese Garden would become a soulless megaplex and a block of high-rise flats would replace the theatre.

Choking back her outrage Emily crammed her nightdress into her bag and zipped it up. All she needed now was her passport. It was in her downstairs desk. She hoped James wasn't still lurking about outside and that she wouldn't be reduced to an undignified scuttling around on bended knees while she searched for it. Carefully closing her bedroom window and drawing the curtains, Emily took one last look around.

Last night's rumpled sheets had been replaced with freshly laundered ones. Emily had tossed and turned into the small hours as her mind churned over all that had happened.

When it was obvious sleep was going to elude her for what remained of the rest of the night, Emily had got up and penned notes to Ted and Ivy, and a general one to all the staff. She decided she would post them on her way to the airport. Emails were too impersonal for what she had to say and she wanted to make sure no-one would read the letters until she was safely out of the country.

She felt bad about letting everyone down and hoped eventually they would realise that she had played no part in the restructuring of the theatre.

Creeping down the stairs, she heard someone rattle the letterbox.

'Emily, dear?' She stifled a sigh at the sound of Miss Simpson's reedy voice. 'Are you all right? I heard shouting and I was worried about you.'

'Miss Simpson?' she called back. 'I'm fine. There's no cause for alarm.'

'Can I let myself in, just to be sure?' There was the sound of a key being turned in the front door lock before Emily had a chance to put her off.

Not for the first time she regretted giving her nosey neighbour her spare key, not that Miss Simpson would have abused her position, but on occasions she let herself into Emily's cottage without checking beforehand if it was convenient.

She always had a ready excuse either a parcel she had taken in for Emily or if she thought Emily had seriously over-slept and would be late for work she came to wake her up. Emily supposed she should be grateful that her neigh-bour cared for her welfare and was such an enthusiastic supporter of neighbour-hood watch, but at times her behaviour could be a tad intrusive — like now.

'Just a minute,' Emily called out.

As she reached the front door a second shadow appeared in the frosted glass behind Miss Simpson and before Emily could take evasive action, James eased past the older woman. Miss Simpson caught unawares was unable to prevent him gaining access.

She gave a little shriek of shock.

'Thank you, Miss Simpson.' James treated her to his most charming smile. 'As you can see Emily's fine and there's nothing for you to worry about. I'll see to things now.'

'Well, really,' Miss Simpson looked very pink in the face as she recovered herself, 'I think perhaps I ought to stay? Emily?' Her pale eyes were bulging with curiosity.

Emily dropped her shoulder bag onto the floor not sure what to do.

'Miss Simpson's very welcome to stay, Emily, but as what I have to say to you is of a rather personal nature, you may wish to ask her to leave. For instance I want to tell you how much I love you and how I can't live without you and these things are better said without an audience don't you agree?'

Miss Simpson turned a deeper shade of pink and began backing out of the doorway.

'I think perhaps I had better go and

see to my cat,' she twittered. 'If you do need me, dear,' she cast her parting shot at Emily, 'I'll be in my kitchen.'

The tiny hall seemed to shrink after Miss Simpson had left.

'Don't come near me.' Emily backed away from James as he made a movement towards her.

'Why not?'

'Whatever it is you've come to say, I don't want to hear it.'

'Well I want a cup of coffee.' James strode past Emily and into the kitchenette. 'I haven't had any breakfast yet and I'm not used to starting the day without my fix of caffeine.'

'Will you please leave?' Emily went after him. 'I have a flight to catch.'

'You're not going anywhere.' James flicked the switch on the jug kettle and began hunting around for mugs.

'This is not your cottage,' Emily protested, 'so stop treating it as your own and stop telling me what to do. You are no longer my boss.'

'Did you sleep well?' James frowned

302

at her. 'No, you didn't, did you? Quite frankly you look a mess.'

'You don't look so wonderful either,' Emily retaliated, noting the shadow of stubble on his chin. 'The belt's twisted on your trousers. Did you get dressed in a hurry?'

'Yes I did, not that it's any business of yours. I've had the nuisance of a job keeping your resignation quiet. I've sworn Tricia to secrecy on pain of death.'

'I wondered how long it would be before you mentioned her name.'

Emily knew that was an unattractive remark to make, but she couldn't ignore the stab of jealousy she felt whenever James mentioned Tricia's name.

'And I had to invent a migraine as the excuse for your sudden departure from the party. Are you jealous of Tricia?' he asked with his most blinding smile.

'No, I am not.' Emily snatched the jar of instant coffee from James and began spooning it into two mugs. Her fingers were shaking and she spilled grains of coffee over the worktop.

'I don't believe you,' James teased her as he watched Emily wipe up the mess. 'And if you are jealous of her that must mean you feel something for me.'

'Will you stop it,' Emily implored, unable to think straight.

She turned on the tap to rinse the cloth and sprayed water down the front of her T shirt.

'Want some help?' James enquired mildly.

'No, I do not.'

'By the way, changing the subject a bit, I think I ought to warn you of the seriousness of your situation.'

'My situation? That's rich coming from you. You're the one who's got some explaining to do. I wouldn't like to be in your shoes when you tell the troops what you've been up to behind their backs.'

'That's as may be, but you ought to know Lottie's threatening to drop by with a lavender something or other to realign your chakras, whatever they are. Ivy's busy looking out her herbal tea remedies for your headache and Tiffany's got some new age therapy stuff she swears by.' James paused with a smile, 'and Tricia whom I suspect didn't believe the headache story for a second says you're to get yourself moving as you've got a theatre to run. Sorry about the abruptness,' he apologised, 'her words not mine.'

'I haven't a clue what you're talking about,' Emily retaliated.

'Then let me try to explain.'

'No, James, don't.' Emily's voice sounded as hollow as she felt. 'I don't want to hear any more of your explanations. You've achieved what you came to West Hampton to do and we have nothing more to say to each other.'

'Exactly what did I come here to do?'

'From the day you arrived you wanted to close the theatre down and develop the site.'

'That's not true.'

'Poor old Lottie must have played straight into your hands when she dreamed up all that nonsense about a ghost called Hamlet.'

'Will you stop talking and let me speak?'

'No.' Emily tossed back her head. 'I thought perhaps after six years away from West Hampton you might have changed for the better but you're still the same two-timing deceiver you always were.'

'I won't dignify that comment with a reply, but as you seem to be in the mood for plain speaking, it's time I had my say. Despite what you think my business interests are not as buoyant as you would have everyone believe. I've had to structure several deals in order to keep the theatre afloat.'

'What does that mean?' Emily snapped.

'Sold properties on if you must know. Investing in The Alhambra stretched my resources to the limit and I realised we were in serious trouble money-wise long before Toby ran off with Carly. I knew that I would have to take emergency action to keep things afloat.'

Emily jumped at the sound of overflowing water and realised the tap was still running. Turning it off created a welcome interruption as she tried to get her thoughts together.

'I approached everyone I could think of to help keep the theatre viable. Joe and Maisie were delighted to help, as was Lottie's ex-husband. He was the first person I approached.'

'I wasn't aware you knew him.'

'I didn't, but Lottie telephoned me after she and Orlando had been going through their address book. She really tore me off a strip saying I couldn't abandon you. I tell you she almost set the telephone lines on fire.'

'Good for Lottie.'

'Like you she seemed to be under the impression my sole aim in life was to close the theatre down. After she'd calmed down a bit, we had a serious talk and came up with the idea of a consortium. Her first husband was well placed to help us out and after that things fell into place.

'Being the actress she is, Lottie was well able to carry off the story she told you about there being a benevolent fund.'

'That still doesn't explain Monty Smith's involvement in all this.'

'He really wants to be part of the local community.'

Emily made a disbelieving noise at the back of her throat.

'You've got to admit he developed Harley's Point with the authorities' approval and without scarring the seafront. He's up for a local award on that one. He doesn't want to rip the soul out of West Hampton he wants to make the best of its marketing opportunities.

'He's shrewd enough to realise The Little Alhambra is one of the resort's best selling points and when I approached him he was more than pleased to offer his help.

'He's promised to keep a back seat

and fully endorses my confidence in you. Tricia's been singing your praises and he values his niece's opinion. He's sorry about all that nonsense at the theatre last night and can only put it down to Orlando's generosity with the liquid refreshment.'

'How very convenient. Perhaps Tricia would like to take over the management of the theatre. She seems to have done everything else required of her.'

James removed the mug of cooling coffee Emily was clutching.

'You don't want that, do you?'

She watched him pour the remains down the sink. He turned back to face her.

'So there you have it. You're expected back at work first thing tomorrow morning. Tiffany and Max are holding tonight's show together and it's business as usual. The box office is working flat out to deal with all the forward bookings. The place is buzzing.'

Unable to meet the expression in James's eyes, Emily turned her head away and glanced out of the window, to where a blinding blue sky promised a beautiful day.

'So where does that leave us?' she asked in an unsteady voice.

'At the risk of offending Miss Simpson's sensibilities,' James moved in closer, 'I really must repeat that I meant every word of what I said in the hall.'

'Miss Simpson?' Emily echoed with a faint frown.

'We can call her as a witness if you like,' James paused with a rueful smile. 'I must admit, I'm not sold on the idea, but,' all traces of the teasing banter left his face, 'if that's what you really want, I'll fetch her over.'

'You said you couldn't live without me.'

'I also said I loved you and have you ever known me lie to you?'

'The theatre?'

'I've explained all that.'

'Lucy Jackson,' Emily persisted.

'Much as I hate to malign a lady, shall we say Lucy was a little economical with the truth about what exactly happened the night she asked me to walk her home?'

'The others?'

'What others? There was no string of broken hearts that summer in West Hampton, at least if there were it was nothing to do with me.'

'What about Tricia?'

'There is no me and Tricia either. There never has been.' James's voice was so soft Emily had to lean forward to hear what he was saying.

'By the way, Toby's another one who bent my ear at the party. He saw you storm out last night and wanted to know what was going on. I tried to explain but he was in no mood to listen and,' James looked most indignant, 'he threatened to run me out of town if I upset you again. I must say,' James added after a short pause, 'your friends are very frank in their choice of threats when they're sticking up for you.'

'We can stand up for ourselves if we're threatened.'

'So I've noticed. Now where does that leave us?'

Emily turned away from the window and slowly put up a hand to stroke the stubble on his cheek. It was rough to her touch.

'I don't know.' Her voice was husky. 'Where does it leave us?'

'Emily, don't walk out on me again.' James's voice sounded as though it hurt him to speak. 'I don't think I could stand it.'

A smile softened her eyes. 'Persuade me to stay. The floor is yours. You've got five minutes to pitch me a line,' she parodied the business style of their first meeting.

'How about if I promise never to visit a fortune-telling booth for the rest of my life. Do you think maybe we could work something out?'

'Possibly,' Emily replied.

'Of course you would have to do your bit too.'

'My bit?'

'You'd have to promise to stay away

from plasterboard and cans of pink paint.'

'I think I could manage that one,' Emily said slowly.

'In that case, we have ourselves a deal, wouldn't you say?'

'You've still got four minutes to go,' she reminded James.

'I could use them telling you how beautiful you are, but I've got a horrid feeling Miss Simpson might start banging on the front door demanding to know what we are up to or Lottie will begin shoving lavender through the letterbox before I've finished. So why don't I just kiss you instead?'

'I think that's a very good idea.' Emily smiled into James's eyes.

As her lips met James's she knew without a shadow of doubt that nothing would ever part them again.